Cipher

Cipher

TONONIYA D.

ARPress
45 Dan Road Suite 5
Canton MA 02021
Hotline: 1(888) 821-0229
Fax: 1(508) 545-7580

Ordering Information:
Quantity sales. Special discounts are available on quantity purchases by corporations, associations, and others. For details, contact the publisher at the address above.

Printed in the United States of America.

ISBN-13:   Softcover   979-8-89356-005-3
            eBook   979-8-89356-006-0

Library of Congress Control Number: 2024902580

DEDICATION

"I would like to dedicate this book to the metamorphosis of everyone that has ever had to experience hurt, pain, or betrayal by someone that was supposed to love and protect them."

She sits there thumb scrolling her touch screen phone. Her attire that of the hip hop culture, Ed Hardy's the devilish wink, accented with a princess cut cross and a sparkling spinner rim watch on a thick red band. Her head high… her lips stained and darkened by the constant smoking of nature's herb and what she calls her escape. Her shoulders as broad as her chest… her locks hanging well below her shoulders, their color as dark as her skin. Her bloodshot eyes trying to focus on the contents of an e-mail that she received from her cast member's bulletin on her next acting role over the internet. Remy's self-proclaimed enemy at her side. Diamond's blonde strains cover the length of her back. While she positions her thin frame next to her warrior's Nubian essence, to ensure that every single sista in here is fully aware that Remy has been bought and paid for… like she is every night by the regulars that frequent the gentleman's club Diamond works at and where they hooked up. Smiling at her small victory over them, she leans in for the kill as she whispers in Remy's ear to get her a drink to quench her thirst and Remy does on command. I feel the steam escape my forehead as I watch Remy hurry back with Diamonds drink in hand. I rehash with Dianah on how Remy just told us a week ago… she had come to an epiphany at the age of twenty-eight and although she had never actually dated a black woman before, she was ready to show the women in her own ethnic background their place and pleasure, because they are queens in her eyes and black women should not only be aware of their royalty but be treated as such. She was crying and all that shit… She was so believable she had Kioni trying to persuade Dianah and me to go out and get some red, black, and green dashikis with her and pump our fists in the air and yell "Power to the People", like most best friends do when they are hyped about something. Now she has the nerve to bring her ass in my house with the trailer park rendition of Malibu Barbie like the conversation never happened. Don't get me wrong, it's not Diamond's dirty blonde hair… blue eyes… nor her fifty dollar body spray that gives her normally pale skin the beautifully brown complexion that she has been telling anyone who will listen she's so proud of… and it's not even the fact that Remy chooses to date white women, that has me hotter than lava. Hell, I kind of understand the reasoning behind my brothers and sisters dating people from different cultural backgrounds. It's sort of like leaving one's country to be recognized as a citizen of the country you just fled. See other cultures are well aware of the strength and royalty that runs through our bloodline and heritage. So in turn, they treat us as such and value our differences. Whereas, we as a culture, are lost and have no idea who we are, let alone uplift each other as a whole. But I am agitated by the fact that African people most often let the propaganda and depiction of our culture lessen their self-worth while they not only run to, but embrace the people or culture that steals everything good about their culture and disguise their true heritage to the point they feel like black is bad. And teach us to hate the very thing that they pay money to emulate. Yeah… we're black and they're beautifully brown. I shake my head and suck my fucking teeth before I take my eyes off Remy's lying ass.

"You know what they say, all the good ones are married…gay, or with white women!" Dianah says, jokingly comparing Remy's potential to the complaints of numerous women that are looking for a man that at the least have a job and treat them with respect. Dianah looks at me with the eyebrow over her right eye cocked up and her lips pressed together like she just took in a smell that her senses didn't agree with.

"Fucking hypocrisy!" Kioni chimes in unexpectedly and the three of us crack up laughing causing everyone to pause what they are in the midst of doing, and all the eyes in the room to center in on us with curiosity.

"Since we have everyone's attention, I would like to know everyone's views on a question that I'm sure you have all been asked at some point, which is how do you label yourself?" I say holding back laughter that's getting harder to control, so I nod my head towards Ebonee, the youngest of the bunch at age twenty one… ok that's putting it mildly… Ebonee is a baby that just put the teething ring down and graduated to whole foods compared to everyone else in our circle… sitting a bowl of my homemade chili and a few pieces of wheat bread down in front of Ivory at the table that's soon to be filled with cards, drinks, and ashtrays. Kioni and Dianah eyes follow my lead just in time to witness Ebonee lean in and kiss her lover Ivory on the lips.

Ivory Dinero is a Computer Software Engineer and more to love in size. If you ask her about her cultural background it varies between Italian... Puerto Rican... Jewish... hell if it's hip to be, she's it. She has wide dark brown eyes with a long thin nose that somehow blends in harmony with her round pale cheeks and curved chin. Her hair is brown with burgundy spikes throughout. She has one gold tooth that is removable and only seems to wear on special occasions, like spade night, and/or any other pride function. At times, she feels the need to perform an impersonation of Mr. T, just with sterling silver jewelry that has been super shined and gives off the uncertainty of whether or not it is silver or platinum. Thank GOD tonight isn't one of them. Her choice of attire consists of expensive designer labels. Every piece of her clothing has to be by the latest popular designer, or she can't wear it, let alone own it. Sometimes, I think she feels that money and material possessions validate her worth. However, she is one of the most loyal friends you could ever ask for and will give you the shirt off her back... when it's beneficial for her. I truly believe that she loves her friends whole heartedly but doesn't know how to separate the object from the emotion when needed. Her smile makes her look like a big old teddy bear, and yes, she's one of those I want to choke the shit out of you one minute and laugh and love the next type of friends. Ivory acts as though Ebonee is not her ideal choice as a lover, but after Cameron's countless reminders that it was her choice to start a relationship with someone as young as Ebonee, Ivory is really working on the way she down plays her affection for her in public, which is only right because we all know that that's not how she treats her when they are alone.

"Ooh I'm Coach all the way!" Diamond says as she holds up her white leather bag covered with rainbow colored C's all over it in one hand and snapping her fingers with attitude with her other hand.

"You know what..." Dianah says shaking her head trying to hold back the laugh that's fighting its way out, as we both fall into each other and the "hell naws" and "no she didnt's" fill the air.

"Hold up y'all before y'all rip her to pieces. She's a newbie. "Let me break it down for you lil' mama," Remy says with her raspy voice, placing her phone on the table in front of her and turning to face Diamond while everyone else finds seats in the living room close around them.

"Labels, as in stud/fem and the dominant breed like myself, my man Cameron, Ivory and Chase, ya feel me?" Remy asks Diamond but really doesn't want her to answer by the way she kept on talking.

"Now peep 'dis. Raven, Kioni, Ebonee, and Dianah are what you call femmes, even though Dianah do both."

"What you mean, she's dominant and femme?" Malibu, I mean Diamond naively questions with a stupid expression on her face. Remy just holds her head in her hands realizing that her attempt to save her just failed miserably.

"The proper terminology is Bi- sexual!" Dianah corrects them both and then rips into Remy. "If you have to tell people my business then make sure you tell it correctly. That's how the misunderstandings and stereotypes of lesbians begin. Some ill-informed person passes on botched information and that same false hood takes on a life of its own!" Dianah says with a bit of a sting in her voice, then takes a sip of her drink.

"Oh I get it. You sleep with both studs and femmes," Malibu says flipping her hair to one side and looking at Dianah with an "I got it" smile.

"Well at least she knows that bi equals two," Kioni says sparking a new wave of laughter.

"Now what did you say you did for a living?" Cameron asks with a torn expression on her face.

"I dance." She replies with a soft giggle. "Y'all should come down to the club with Remy and Ivory sometimes. They have ladies night every Friday. And that means y'all don't need no male escort to get in." Cameron rubs her right hand slowly across the back of her head, which is a clear sign that my wife is fighting to keep her opinion to herself.

"You sure know how to pick 'em Remy." Dianah pats Remy on her shoulder bringing the heat of everybody's eyes that Remy was trying to avoid, directly to her.

"A college degree is not required for that position," Remy snaps.

"But you would think some level of education would be needed to hold a position beside you. But obviously not." Dianah adds another wound to Remy's bruised ego.

"It's not that complicated. Sometimes she feels like having a nut and sometimes she doesn't!" Ebonee blurts out without reserve as she leaned in close and touched Diamond's hand, like they are sharing an intimate girl moment at a slumber party hosted by Betty Boo.

"Like you said Dianah, some ill – informed person tries to fucking inform somebody and has no factual data to back up the shit they are saying!" Ivory shoots a piercing glance at Ebonee to make sure she knows she's the ill- informed person she is referring to.

"No you didn't go there, Ivory!" Chase calls Ivory on her insult, then the both of them start cracking up without regard for Ebonee's feelings what-so-ever.

"Ok, pay up… I want my money right now! I knew she wouldn't get through the hour without a sarcastic condescending comment towards her." Kioni says holding out her hand to collect the money owed to her.

"Oh you guys bet on me and shit?" Ivory questions .

"Damn right!" We all say in unison as I hand over the fifty dollar pot.

"Thanks babes," Kioni says as she kisses Ivory on the cheek to show her appreciation for the early jabbing and put the cash in her bra and patted it for safe keeping.

"Any way." I say laughing and bring the conversation back to the topic. "Let me make this clear for you Diamond. In the gay community there are several classifications of lesbians… Some in which are the ones that go by no classification, Femmes, Aggressive femmes, Studs, Butches, and just plain Dominant women. All who know that they are women, but prefer certain things in and out of the bedroom. I would be labeled a "femme"… short for feminine of course," I glance over at Diamond. "The label of femme is supposed represent the "role" I play in a relationship… my style of dress… and even the capacity to which I show my emotions… Even though the capacity at which I show great emotion has nothing to do with a label, and everything to do with who I am as a woman. So if the "role" of femme is to be submissive at all times like some would imply… then that label really doesn't fit me… In my opinion people should keep the labels where they were meant to be…. on clothes!" I try to explain as simplified as I possibly can so she can understand.

"I agree, labels of any kind should be eradicated! I, for one, no longer use classifications to define myself or the attraction that I have for women… even though society and our own community labels us based off of their own perceptions of what they think we should be as lesbians and most of us at some point and time went along with the labels because we were not only trying to find out who we were, but someone, anyone that we could identify with. I guess to a certain degree people are still searching because they have still placed a label on me, I am a NO CLASSIFICATION!" Chase glances at her long term lover Kioni before she shakes her head and throws her hands in the air.

"That is so true. When I came out the labels helped me understand who I am. I love being a femme. I think that it fits me because I'm super girly. I would die without my makeup, nails, and shopping!" Ebonee says with animated enthusiasm.

"Wow, placing me under a label for any reason is hard for me to do because this is real life for me and being a lesbian is just a small part of what makes me who I am. The same as being the head nurse of a trauma unit, or being a mother, or a lover. I am a woman with a real family that deals with real problems. But with that being said if I absolutely have to define myself with a label, I will say an aggressive femme because although I am very feminine, when it comes down to the things that I do with my lover, I have and can become very aggressive." Kioni says with a mischievous laugh because she knows that she has shared all of those aggressive deeds in detail with Dianah and me, her besties.

"I'm a dominant woman with a bald head. I don't change the tone in my voice… I don't alter my appearance in any way to emulate a man, nor do I desire to be one. But because I don't wear makeup and I prefer to wear a t-shirt that happens to come off of the male rack opposed to the form fitting ones on the female rack, I have somehow forfeited my womanhood and been thrown into the box of transgender by society, addressed as "bro" or "my man" by men and other aggressive females as a sign of respect on their part, automatically called daddy by women that find me attractive as though that is supposed to excite me in some way, and branded a "NO TOUCHER", just because I enjoy using a strap by the woman in our community without anyone ever asking me who I am or what it is that I like!" Cameron says with a look of intensity on her face.

"I'm a hard stud, all the way! Ya'll knows I'm that female with a nigga swag, so I love it when they call me big papa," Ivory's voice deepens on the word papa and we all burst out laughing for different reasons, mine being I doubt if she has ever been hard a day in her life.

"As for me, I'm Raven, a thirty-four-year-old psychiatrist and the host of tonight's event. A few friends of mine and I throw a get together once a month where we play spades… cook or cater… have a few drinks and release the stresses of our month with some mentally stimulating debatable conversations… some laughter… hell even at times shedding some tears. We don't always agree with each other's ideals or opinions, but I know that there is a form of strength that comes by just being open to different points of views. The openness that we share causes a gradual demise of ignorance and shines a light of knowledge, which allows positive change, healing, and soul elevation in each of our lives when it's all said and done, whether we know it at the time or not.

Raven Winters-Carver

I am a product of a woman's love and a man's miss definition of the same. I grew up in a house with revolving doors that my father used often and my mother never changed, no matter how painful his infidelities. And it wasn't because she was uneducated, jobless, or unattractive that she allowed him to take from her soul at will. In fact, she was the exact opposite of all three. It was because she was his wife, for better or for worst. She was his wife.

That's what she told me the day I came home with my shirt drenched with tears and my eyes swollen from wiping them away because my best friend and I walked in on her mother and my father having sex on their kitchen counter one summer day. I didn't know which hurt worse, my father's actions or my mother's devotion to him, even after telling her what I had been witness to. I was certain that marriage was never going to be in my future if marriage meant I had to accept my husband's constant and blatant disrespect... In fact what I saw confirmed the feelings that I had been having about girls even more. I didn't know how to go about acting on my feelings at the time but I did know I never wanted to have a man touch me the way I saw my father touching my best friend's mother.

As the years went by I did everything in my power to make sure love was not in the cards for me by ending all of my relationships before the demands of love had a chance to begin. So I went through my fair share of emotionless relationships with women. All of which were sexually gratifying to me and only engaged in when they were convenient for me. Then I met her, Cameron's slanted light brown eyes reap with seduction. Her lips are the type that you find yourself wanting to feel all over your body. Cameron Carver taught me how to escape the grasp the stickiness that emotions sometimes get trapped in. With each glance she extended her hand and offered me the chance of new possibilities with her by my side. Then a few months after dating, I was listening to Cameron perform a piece called Shattered Reflection on the stage at Voodoo lounge. The words to the poem were like tiny mirrors aimed at my soul. And the words I was studying hard to obtain my degree in psychology with, hit me. I realized that I had not become my mother; a woman tied to a man by nothing more than a state stamped document. I had become the acts of my father; involved with an entourage of women that were meaningless to me and that I was not proud of. I decided that I was going to break the cycle that I have inherited. I was going to invest in myself the commitment that my father never had for my mother and I. I'm going to replace the respect that each one of his publicized relationships stripped from me. I will deal with the understanding that my parents are humans with flaws. I will build the strength needed to mend my own wounded soul. So I'll do what I swore off years ago and that leaves not only me but every human being the most vulnerable, I'll love. I'll love in a new way from what I've seen growing up. I'll love in a way that's always true to me. I'll love the way love is supposed to be and that's freely. I'll love through all my imperfections as tattered as I may be.

Cameron lays her head on my right shoulder, draping her hand across my left breast causing my heart beat to magnify inside my own head. The space in our California king size bed covered in deep brown earth tone sheets, was enough for at least two more naked bodies to rest comfortably next to us. But here we are just the two of us after ten years of playful banter with each other about who occupies the majority of the bed with their sprawled limbs… right smack dab in the center of the bed looking each other in the eyes smiling and greeting each other with soft good morning kisses, the same as every morning even when one of us remains in the bed longer than the other. When it comes to my wife, I suffer from a syndrome that I like to call 'brains on the pillow' (that's when you are in the state of euphoria usually after an orgasmic release and it leaves you without the ability to think rationally) and oh how my senses leak… Her unconditional love makes my heart stronger than it's ever been… and my body all so weak. I hear her voice and I'm off track and completely focused at the same time. She is my addiction and no matter how high I get when I consume her, her essence always seems to take me higher. I'm torn from my insecurities that once had me running from commitments of the heart now protected in her embrace. Cameron makes me wild, bold, and uninhibited as she tames, claims, and renames me in her love. She redefines what love and the actions of being in love are to me every day. And even though I met Cameron ten years ago and became the number one lady in her life and she in mines, at times my assurance in her love and cool demeanor betray me, and so do my degrees. And I am left a woman, a woman that wants to be everything for her lover. And in those moments my mind, body, and soul battles in a silent war between the ugly question that is embedded deep within my subconscious, along with love's emotions that I fall into without warning. And I hear the voice inside my head saying the words, am I enough?

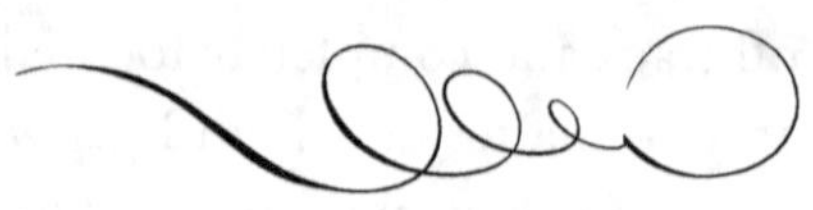

Ivory Dinero

The thundering sound of the car door rang through the air as loud as the pop of the window. The window shattered, spewing particles of glass all over the tan leather interior in my Arctic white C-280 Mercedes Benz, my hair, and the empty parking spot next to mine.

"You broke my fucking window you fucking bitch! You broke my got damn window. You're gonna pay for that!" I jumped out the car after Ebonee. She was walking so fast that she was almost at the front door.

"It's not your fucking car!" she snaps at me, as she digs her curly tipped acrylics covered with rhinestones and bright colors inside the Gucci bag that I bought her, and pulls out her keys.

"I only have thirty-six payments left and it's mine!" I yell even though we were face to face.

"And I'm supposed to be the fucking ill-informed one… right!" She laughs in my face which adds insult to injury and I lash out.

"You are, you dumb bitch." I say then I smack her so hard that her fucking wet and wavy pony tail shifts to one side of her head. I unlock the door, enter into my two bedroom town house to get the broom and dust pan out of the storage closet in the solarium, to clean up her fucking mess and I hear the door slam behind me and I turn to face her. Her usual smooth deep brown complexion seems to have darkened to the darkness of her eyes. Her lips sustain a swollen fullness as they are force into a grimace. Ebonee uses every bit of her thickness to her advantage as she charges at me full of rage. She grabs me by my hair and punches me in my face. We are no longer lovers, nor are we strangers to this moment, where nothing is like we dreamed it would be, when we were caught up in each other's smile… cared about each other's happiness… interested in each other's dreams… or high from the feelings after our first kiss… and our fist fly like venom and we fight to breathe.

I look at my face in my full wall bathroom mirror and I hate my reflection. My left eye is already turning black and blue. My right eye is split over the eye socket on the right side. My nose is covered in smeared blood and my bottom lip is busted and swollen. I reach in the medicine cabinet and sit all the supplies I am gonna need to patch myself up on my brown and white marble bathroom counter.

"Fuck!" I yell out as I feel the sting of the alcohol in my open wound and my soul. "How did I get here? Is this all that I am worth? The hype of an idea… the idea of having a woman that can buy them what they want… the idea of having a kid, a house, a family. I am a fucking idea… trashed by the responsibility of reality. My life, my reality, is that I was never really wanted… and if I was wanted, that want was not enough to keep her fucking ass from putting me in a dirty brown paper bag and rolling me into the center of a got damn shopping mall and leaving me there two weeks after I was born.

My own mother left me wrapped in a raggedy towel in the largest strip mall in Florida and walked away. Sometimes I stand in the center of the mall and try to imagine her franticly looking for the woman with eyes like hers or the man that fathered me. Then I say fuck it and fuck her for abandoning me and I go shopping… not because I want to, but because I can… in fact, I own clothes from every store in that fucking mall and so does my girl, although she has no idea that I was left there 36 years ago.

And at times like these I am glad that I didn't tell Ebonee the whole truth about my life. Glad that I didn't tell her how I bounced around from foster home to foster home. From the ones that took in orphans to increase their bank accounts and didn't give a shit about the kids… to the ones that barely fed me because they sold the food stamps for cash so they could get high… to the ones that had drinking problems, so they were quick to take out their aggravation on me. Until I reached eighteen, and was given a check for two hundred and fifty dollars, my freedom, and a folder that contained four pieces of paper that told me who I was. The first one was my admission paper that listed me as "Jane Doe", how old I appeared to be, where it was that Officer Watts, the security guard on duty, found me and my condition at the time. Next was a birth certificate that read Ivory Dinero. Someone's joke I'm sure. Mother was listed as unknown and under the word guardian was a red 'ward of the state of Florida' stamp, behind that laid my social security card. And last but not least, the last sheet read release on her eighteenth birthday… that date had the same date as my admission paper only eighteen years later, December the fifteenth. I stuffed the folder in my Jansport backpack next to the yellow envelope that contained my full scholarship to Lynn University in the fall.

I drop the soiled cotton balls, q- tips, and gauze in the trash can and clean out the sink and wipe down the counter. I look myself in the eyes. I can handle this… But I could never take her or anyone else throwing this shit in my face whether it's the truth or not. It's definitely not an option, so I create the idea of having the kid, the house, the family that was taken when I was left alone and I do give the woman in my life what they want, even if I have to purchase it on credit. I turn out the light, open the door and make my way to the living room.

"I already cleaned out the car and swept the glass from the parking lot. I put a piece of cardboard in the window to keep anything from getting in the car until morning, when you can take it to get it fixed." Ebonee says from the couch and then goes back to her prior conversation she was having on her cell phone.

"Ok…" I mutter. I really want to check and make sure that my car is secure but I know that my doing so would be a whole other battle within itself that I'm just not up for. So I just walk to my bedroom and turn in for the night.

Dianah Marshall

I'm taken away by the beauty and symmetry of a piece called 'Divided'. I stand in front of it my eyes searching each line as it contrasts into the next. I let the colors pull me into the emotion that Sahara, a talented South African artist, was feeling when she created it. I wonder if she was as torn in that moment as I am in this one. I wonder if the battle expressed within her unframed portrait was the same that was in my heart, the battle between self-truth and social normalcy.

Truth, I ran away from Carla because she wanted a relationship when we both agreed to have fun. Truth, I can't commit to a relationship without love and I was never in love with her. Did I want to… truthfully… yes. But what would my life be like waking up to a woman and coming home at the end of the day to the same. My mother was right, that's something I do for fun. That's what she told me when I told her I had sexual feelings for a girl so many years ago, before dismissing the concept and me. So I leave women as that, fun, and I run from my truth into the always welcoming, always waiting arms of my college sweetheart and the only male lover I have ever had, Vance. Vance Hunter, my two hundred and fifty pounds of masculine diesel. With his large hands with veins that stand out as prominently as his pussy eating lips, strong jaw line, and deep, almond shaped dark brown eyes. I've always been honest and forthcoming with him about my dealings with women since the day we started dating. Yet he still adores the woman he sees in me. He is an ebony thoroughbred that works out daily and his body is the perfect specimen of a man, of social normalcy.

"Stunning!"

"I couldn't agree with you more." I reply to the English accent as I slowly remove my sight from the masterpiece and on to the canvas of a slender ebony skin woman that looks as though she has come straight from the motherland with her high cheek bones that stood to the right of me. Her hair feathered her face on the left side and lay behind her ear on the right, settling just pass her shoulders. She was wearing a casual but dressy white collar blouse with black trim along the V-neck and down the front of it, matching the black of her wide leg dress pants that fell to the center of her black leather open toe five inch heels perfectly.

"The artwork is impressive, but I was referring to you and your state of intensity." She complimented with a confident forwardness.

"I'm flattered but I think you're only fascinated because it's admired from a distance." I laugh.

"I'm Ramona…"

"Ndiaye" I finished her introduction with the correct pronunciation of her last name (Na- Day). I didn't know her by sight, but her name was on the pamphlet that gave a brief summary of the wealthy philanthropist's love for the arts and her culture, which compelled her to fund the art show tonight. She smiled exposing her beautifully aligned white teeth. She reached out her hand to shake mine.

I did the same.

"Dianah Marshall."

"I doubt that highly. Allow me the opportunity of removing the distance by taking you out."

Her thick tone is a smooth cocktail of eroticism and intrigue that I slowly sip as she enunciates her words clearly, stretching each syllable to an exact length.

"An inviting temptation but I don't think that would be a good idea."

"Why not?"

"Honestly, I'm in a relationship with a man at the moment." I searched her demeanor for the classic "you're bi-sexual" predilection that's always laced with disgust, like I fuck a multitude of unclean, unnamed men in filthy alley ways back to back, don't bathe, and put the mixed DNA in my female lover's mouth deceitfully. But it didn't change. Instead she steps closer to me, gives me a sultry glance and says…

"I would love to get to know the woman that equates the intensity!"

"And in another place and time Ms. Ndiaye, I would love to see if you could withstand the very thing you desire when given in its entirety. But a want does not make it accessible. It was very nice meeting you." I say just before I blend into the crowd.

I call Vance on the phone. I tell him that I'm fifteen minutes away from his one bedroom waterfront condo inside the Player's Club Estates and that I was on my way over. The idea of waking up to me in his arms put him in a cogent mood.

Vance and I have been back together four months now and he wants to ensure a stable future together, as he put it, and solidify things by moving in together, something we have never done in the past. But I like having my own space, so I keep my own place an hour away from his. I'm close enough to get to but far enough that he calls to make sure I am home before he travels the distance. I unlock the door with my key and enter his spacious contemporary living room that's furnished with clear glass and mirrors. He accented it with slate gray curtains and lampshades that matched his couch of the same color. The air fills my nose with the scent of Life, an oil base air freshener that I am fond of. I walk down the hall to the bedroom where the sound of movement tells me he is.

Vance closes the charcoal dresser draw to his lacquer set, with his white t-shirt in his hand. I walk over to him before he puts it over his head. I place my left French manicured hand inside the front of his white boxer briefs and cup what has been given to me before running my fingers along its length. I place my tongue in his mouth gaining his attention with its warmth, making sure that he is clear on what I want and where I need him to take me. By scratching the nails of my right hand slowly down the back of his bald head, broad neck, chiseled back, then his tight ass, where I dig in and is adding to his stimulation. He kneads my neck with his tongue, grips my dark brown blouse where it reveals my cleavage and rips it open sending the buttons that once held it together flying across the Brazilian walnut floor. His aggression is fuel for my inferno. I fling off my beige and brown Gucci shoes while he unbuttons my beige straight leg cut pants leaving my panties on stuck to my center's glue. I stop him as he tries to pick me up and lay me on top of his king size bed to prep me with his tongue. Instead I get on my knees reach in the nightstand for one of the Magnum Ecstasy's out of the box of thirty minus two I placed there and always use with him since day one. I throw it back at him. He grabs it and tears it open with his teeth. He rolls the condom until it runs out of rubber on his excitement. He adds more lube to the pre-lubrication. He unglues my Secret's, pulling them to the right; he takes my hair into his hand drawing me on to him as he thrust himself into me.

I let out a gasp of contentment as he makes entry.

"Damn, you feel so good, so tight, open up for me, take me all the way this time baby!" He says with his rugged tone, as he goes deeper trying to make me do just that.

He is so thick that I grasp the blanket and press my face into its plush to conceal my grimace. He spreads my cheeks apart, eases out, then slowly creeps back in. He knows my body, knows that feels good to me.

"Mm mm…" I moan gently and move my hips softly letting him know that we are in sync with each other's desire. We dance to the music of lovers that our bodies create. I make him slippery once, twice…

"Shit, yeah, work with me, like that." He says grinding as he places his thumb in my second treasure, causing his pleasure to throb and me to make him slippery for the fourth time.

"Fuck me!" he ordered, then assist my change in tempo and his level of depth by forcing me on him completely by my waist.

"Ooh…" I inhale hard and his breathing picks up.

"Yeah, fuck me!"

"Ouch!" I squeal in a high pitch unable to mask my emotions as he makes me take all of him at this point.

I call out to him to remind him of his strength and size. "Ooh… baby… Ooh…"

"I'm gonna… cum so hard… Jodye!" he said as he jerks deep inside my center.

"Jodye? Who the hell is Jodye? Vance?" I question vehemently as I push his limp muscles away from me.

"That's not important."

"Not important? You're inside my body and calling out another woman's name! I definitely think it is of importance!"

"I didn't mean to do that."

"Who in the hell does?" I cut my eyes at him.

"I am sorry. It was a slip of the tongue, that's all. What can I do to make it up to you and convince you that you are the only woman I want in my life?" he touches my chin.

"Convince me?" I yell, not out of jealousy because we both date other people when we were not together, but because of the principle. I get up and gather my clothing and shoes, putting them back on as I make my way to the front door, with Vance at my heels.

"Dianah, please don't leave like this!"

"So you do remember my name after all." I say as I pick up my keys and walk out the door and make my way to my car, my home, and my shower.

Chase James

I watch you in your sleep and wonder if I am still the one you see in your dreams, because you are still here with me after broken promises, you simply say you love me, yet I feel so incomplete. I try to tell you I don't want to exist like this, engulfed in the highs of your smile and laughter for months without end to have them erased by combined minutes of pain but the words get stuck in my throat and I swallow them. I never meant to be that monster that you fear lurking in the dark. I never meant to be a fucking woman beater. I don't even know when things changed from us talking about any and everything openly and honestly. I don't know why the hitting starts; I never meant to hurt you. I love you. I love the life we use to share and the one we can have, but is the love in my heart enough to heal the pain I've caused? I inhale your peace from the air and ask you in your ear softly, "what is love in its purest form and why is the action of love so hard to do?"

I heard the words whispered through tears, yelled in rage, and I have spoken them so many times that I know they've lost their value with you. I wish you could validate my loves' worth. I move away from her side and fight my tears. Maybe loves value never had a chance to grow, because it was always spoken through the lips of vultures as they were chewing my flesh. Funny how love can be so shallow and superficial or it can cut so deep. And when thoughts of you flash across my mind, I go insane thinking that my stupidity could cause me to lose you. Cause me to lose my son. Cause me to be by myself in this world of chaos. I am sorry for everything I've done to hurt you. I know I love you and I know that things have to change. You mean the world to me and I want your heart. I want to replace the tears in your eyes with gleam. I want to replace my yelling and I want to destroy your screams.

I want to love you… plan and simple. I want to love you without the words being said… I want to love you, Kioni.

"I love you…" my mother said as she wiped my tears and let hers fall behind the drawn curtain of the same emergency room that I have been treated in numerous times throughout my childhood. I said nothing in response to her display of affection towards me as the Percocet numbed the pain from my fractured ribs and split gum that exposed the root of my tooth before the stitches. The same way she kept silent every time my father placed his damn hands on me. See, My father isn't an alcoholic or a drug addict of some sort. My daddy is a decorated police officer with honors that lace the walls of our living room and family den. He just doesn't like the fact that he fathered me, a girl of no worth. And when he found me on top of another girl in my bedroom at fifteen he lost it. I could never carry on his name or in his mind even be able to continue the family tradition and be the fourth generation to wear a shield. I will prove him wrong. The same way I do with my answers every time the doctor asks the cause of my afflictions after one of his fits of rage and I reply sports is the cause.

"The broken arm?" the emergency room physician questioned with concern as he read from a medical chart that listed injuries form per visits here.

"Football." I answered him with the same answer listed on the paper in his hand.

"Dislocated shoulder?"

"Basketball."

"Broken nose?"

"Hockey." I watch the tension line form in the doctors forehead as he gives up on me confiding in him the truth.

"Ok… Mrs. James, I strongly suggest that you encourage your daughter to find a no contact extracurricular activity!" he said as he handed her my discharge papers and perceptions with a look of distain on his face. He walked out the room and so did we.

I walk across the platform with my head held high. My hat at the right angle, my blues pressed crisp, and my shoes shined so deep that you can see the clouds in them. But most of all I could feel the weight of my fire arm on my side and the warmth of the steel badge in my hand. I am his walking contradiction. I am what he never thought I would be…or could be… Officer James, the fourth generation of officers. In this moment, I am what I always wanted to be, a glimmer of hope in my daddy's eyes.

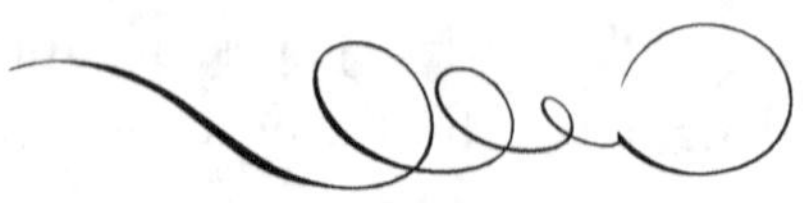

Ebonee Price

I replay the image of your smile. Listen hard to the silence that fills the empty space between your happiness and mine. And hear the words 'I love you' fade into pain and disappointment. I sacrifice many nights in the cold alone, no family to turn to, because I confessed to them that it was you I loved. And because I love a woman I'm hated by ignorant people in the world that define my existence by miss information of homosexuality and the last girl on girl scene in a raunchy low budget porn tape created by a man to fulfill the fantasy of a man that they have seen. People don't judge me based on my character, they don't even take the time to know me as a person before they condemn me to hell for touching a woman and deepen their despised for me even more for choosing you, and not someone of my own ethnicity. And it's both painful and ironic that the ignorance doesn't skip the homosexual community or our families!

"Dem fuk over we Afrikaans and steal we education and land. Meh tell yuh one time, if yuh flex with dah wretched cunt, don't come check meh yuh, nah welcome seen!" My mother was so enraged, she yelled out in both Patois and English two years ago as I gathered the few belongings I owned to take with me to Ivory's place. The distain in her voice made my heart hurt and my heart was to blame for my mother's heart ache because I loved you.

I love you more than you ever loved me. It's as evident to my eyes now as the fifth teen year difference in age is to everyone we come in contact with. The same difference in age that you said didn't matter because you were in love with me and I believed you. I had no reason not to you made me feel like I was the most beautiful woman in the world. You use to talk to me about your dreams and really listen to me when I shared mine with you. You made me feel like nothing was out of reach especially not you, but lately you're always preoccupied. I love you and you act like you don't want me here anymore. I try to make ordinary moments special with you again, but if we're not having sex then your time is too much to give me. So I take the moments given to me, I fulfill your every desire even the ones that make me uncomfortable and I know your satisfied because of the things you let me do to you in return. But out of bed, you are so cold and I don't even know the you, the you turn into. The love between us is dying more and more each day because we no longer say or do the things that we need to or for each other. Our world is crumbling around us and it seems like the only one that cares is me.

I wear a smile when my heart is broken in two because I'm not dumb nor am I the naive little girl that you make me out to be whenever we are out with your friends. I was just foolish enough to think that the lies you fed me behind closed doors had some truth. I needed to believe the words you said had truth! So I let you make me look small so that your ego could remain large… In hopes that you and the love you once had for me would come back to me… But sadly the naive little girl is you, because someone watches me from a distance and she is getting closer to me each day. She laughs and flirts with me, makes me feel desired. She's not only interested but she's attentive to me, when you look right through me. She wipes the tears that you've placed on my face away; her words are up lifting and free of judgment. You don't care if I go, she tells me that if you don't want me, she does and pleads with me to stay. Ivory, your actions don't deserve me and she's eager to fill your shoes. She wants me the way that you have me… and had me since day one, and you could care less. She says that she is more than willing to show and prove her desire for me, and I'm beginning to form a desire for more than you. Her indecent proposals for me to give her the chance and her affection for me will outweigh the tide of you being my first are getting stronger. Maybe she's right after being with her I will no longer feel the need to hold on to you… In her touch, as casual as it has been, lies all of the emotion that use to be and I wish were still in yours. Baby, my body is pulling me towards her while my heart keeps me with you. I miss you… I miss your laughter… I miss your jokes… I miss the way you made me feel safe in your arms…I miss you loving me…You are the only woman that has had me, so I keep her at bay and reach for you. I reach for you with the hope that you will feel my love and reach for me in return… And you turn away. Damn you for turning away each time I reach out to you. Ivory, I'm tired of being alone whenever you're not inside of me. I'm tired of feeling unwanted when you claim you need me. I'm tired of pleading my love into your deaf ears. I'm tired of being taken for granted when I know that there is at least one person out there in the world that wants me. I'm tired of holding on to the good we once had because I'm not the only one in this relationship. My body is tired and my hands are rope burnt from this emotional tug of war of the heart… so I'm letting go.

Remy Gamble

Tonight is one of those nights that I want to sleep in my own bed. I picked Diamond up from work, and dropped her off at her spot right after we hit an ATM. She promised to break me off so I would have something to lace my pockets with. My parents are gone on vacation for two weeks so I have the joint to myself. I'm glad because it's way past my curfew of midnight. My old girl kept me in mind and made me a big pan of lasagna before she left. "I love you moms…" I say out loud like she could hear me. I pop a plate in the microwave and grab a beer out the fridge.

Ok I'll be the first one to admit that I'm spoiled rotten, but isn't every woman supposed to be? I love and thank my parents for loving me to the fullest. I can show you childhood pictures that prove they have always loved me to the fullest since the day I was born. They never let me want for anything and always kept me with the finer things in life, even when I came out, ya feel me? From shoes, clothes, jewelry, to my 1969 winter green Chevy Camaro, with white racing stripes on the hood. I love my baby! I shake my head at the thought of me behind the wheel. And my pops keeps underneath the hood on point. He has me bring it into the family shop every month.

My pops is the Mack of Mack's, a true old school ladies' man. He be dressed to impress at all times. And the ladies be on it. Whoa, I wanna be like my old man when I grow up. I'm not that far away now. My phone is full of numbers, and my lil man stays in the shade. I grip the print of my strap between my legs and think about all the places we've been together. And my old girl, she's beautiful. Even though she's in her sixties, she's the flyest woman I know. If I didn't know her age, I would swear she was in her forties…. Her skin is smooth and clearer than some of these busted ass females that be on my dick. Man, when my moms and pops step out, my old girl be looking classy. But I haven't found one chic that can hold a candle to the love my old girl has for me and shares with my pops. So imma just keep doing what I do; meeting, sleeping, and creeping; Playing these hoes before they play me. Ya gotta love the fans. I know I do. Every time they run up on me and drop them digits, it brings a smile to a nigga face and their pussies to my room, even if it's only for one night. I know you think I'm foul for saying that, but the truth is the truth. Hell, the only reason I'm privy to first night fucks is because they see me in a movie or catch one of my plays, thinking they gonna get their hands on my paper stacks. Dumb hoes, I ain't even gettin' paid yet! I'm just working towards a goal, trying to get my face and name out there. Hell, don't hate, I give them what they are really after… their 15 minutes in the limelight! Not to say that 'just sex' doesn't get boring… But who was it that said 'All the world's a stage?' Well, I'm an actor dammit! I laugh, take a swig of my beer, and turn on the pc.

I check my email, fan page, and scroll through all the friends' comments that were posted on my social network site. Then the chime of my messenger came in with half the message, "Hey u... what …" displayed on the bottom right corner from ThickMrs.21, then vanishes into the blinking icon on my taskbar. I click open the messenger box.

ThickMrs.21: Hey u… what u been up 2 lately?

DoULike2Gamble: Just getting my hustle on… u know how I do

ThickMrs.21: Yeah… I know what u mean … I'm surprised 2 even c u online

DoULike2Gamble: Yeah… checking my mail & u know I gotta keep up with my fans. Cuz without them… there's no me…lol

ThickMrs.21: O boy… here u go on that ego trip of urs… but I like it…lol☺

DoULike2Gamble: Is that so? & how much do u like it?

ThickMrs.21: I like it a lot daddy. U know that shit makes me wet! I miss u so much… I need 2 feel u

DoULike2Gamble: U wouldn't have 2 miss me if u would stop playin' with a nigga… you know I fucks with you the long way!

ThickMrs.21: I'm not playin' with you… I'm ready 2 do this….

DoULike2Gamble: Ur ready?

ThickMrs.21: I been ready… It was just hard for me to… you know…

DoULike2Gamble: Ok peep dis… if u ready & I make that pussy wet, y don't u reach down there & touch it 4 me

ThickMrs.21: Ur 2 late boo… already there!

DoULike2Gamble: Taste it 4 me then…

ThickMrs.21: Mmmm…. So sweet… u don't know what u missin'

DoULike2Gamble: So just how soon can I find out?

ThickMrs.21: Sooner than u think…. U can meet me

DoULike2Gamble: Where @? Ur crib or a hotel?

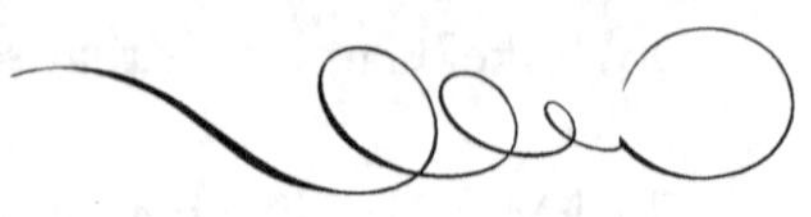

Kioni Wils

"They raped me… I never spoke those words. How do I tell my son, my beautiful imperfection, that he is either the son of a wealthy man that had his wealth passed down to him along with his horrible actions, or that he is the son of the intelligent wealthy guru himself? Would the truth eat away at all the purity inside of him? Would he hate himself? Even worse, would his love and affection for me mutate into hate and disgust?" I rub the palm of my hand against my throbbing temple and I keep talking. "I told Deshaun that I was madly in love with a classmate named Hatethem and one day, and one time, although we were too young at the time, we gave in to the color difference and created him. I lied to him, I lied to you, I lied to cover many lies. I turned myself into what they called me, a fast ass girl, and even though it was only in the eyes of my mother and her husband, it felt easier to feed that image to my son than telling the truth. When I realized that the pain I was feeling wasn't the residual from their nightly assaults, but contractions… that's what he called me. A fast ass girl… My mother believed him because it was easier to face than the fact that I, my body, was of little sacrifice, worth the wealth that came from her husband. And Deshaun believed me because I'm his mother, imperfect, flawed, but enough for him… enough for her… but how could she rape me?" Tears streamed from my eyes, merging at my chin, dropping to random parts of my thighs with the weight of golf ball size hail in a storm.

"Who…who are they… who raped you?" Raven questions with controlled worry. I can tell by the expression on her face that she is trying to stay focused on the words I'm saying and not let her emotion of rage that accompanies the word rape, compliments of her profession, take over and change the mood of two friends into an abused woman and a counselor as I continue.

"It's over, Kioni?" Chase asked me in a low voice, which I knew was the calm before the storm as her eyes shift from me to the open suitcase that contains some of my gathered clothes.

"Yes." I looked at my lover and saw the rage in her eyes that I have come to know all too well, but before I could maneuver myself out of harm's way, Chase hit me with an open back hand across the right side of my face that knocked me off my feet. I could taste the blood in my mouth as I landed on the one place in our home and relationship that had never succumbed to violence until this moment. In the seconds that it took me to refocus, Chase was already reaching her hand in-between my legs, ripping my panties away from my body.

My soul felt the weight of a thousand souls broken and battered by false hoods. Then came the flashes of past pain… memories… living… reawakened from their dungeon. Flash, flash, flash… the off white palm of the first hand of abuse in my life appears … a hand so big that it covered not only my mouth to contain my screams but my nose, and half of my eyes. Leaving only the corners to take in the sight of my mother's husband, that I was told to call daddy. His pale face was filled with sexual satisfaction along with his grunts. His fingers laced my forehead, the tips resting beyond my soft hairline. As he caused me so much hurt, so much hurt down there where pee-pee and boo-boo come out.

"Baby, please… baby, no ouch" I cry out to Chase before I have another flash back.

Flash, flash, flash… "That's how you do it boy… just like that!" The voice of my mother's husband fills my head as he guided his sixteen-year-old son's violation inside my body like I was a blow up doll in a fucking sex education class.

"This shit… we aren't over… till I say it's over… this pussy … you… will always belong to me!" You will always belong to me… those are his words coming from my lovers' mouth and her voice brought me back to the now.

"Oh God…Oh God … No…Not you… Not this… Chase… stop…baby please… stop… no… anything but this…!" I tried to push her off of me…force her from inside of me, out of my womb… tried to reverse the wrong that was being done before it was completed. But Chase was to strong, or my soul had become too weak, too broken, to fight. So with the next ram intended to inflict pain on my body, I allowed myself to slip away from her the way I taught myself to slip away from them… slip away from this pain… slip away from this betrayal… slip away … slip far away. I exited out of my body leaving the shell that has been invaded and tortured, too many times to give an accurate count, but never by a woman … never by her. And I floated over myself… and hovered… over us… I watched my lover that was always compassionate when it came to sex and lovemaking. Chase was always gentle, pleasing, and all so convincing that although she was physically abusive at times, she loved me. Her embrace always told me that she loved me. That she was in love with me… with every kiss… every embrace… every bonding moment shared through pleasure Showing me that there was a difference between forced penetrations and making love. And she only made love to me."

I tilt my head towards Raven and reveal myself to my friend.

"I watched the muscles of her half-covered ass cheeks tighten then release over and again. As she cut into my inner tissue with her strap on, causing a stream of blood to flow down my thigh and bleed into the white linen sheets. I watched Chase grab my neck… the same neck that she places passion marks on as she reached her climax. I watched her grope my breast roughly underneath the purple sundress I was wearing. I watched her tongue pry my lips apart and take my bottom lip into her mouth before she partook in a one sided kiss. I watched the way love transformed into disgust, sealed with life's most powerful adhesives, Blood and Tears."

I watch Raven's tear filled face as she walks over to me and holds me tight. She doesn't say anything she just holds my hand and sits next to me.

"I should have told Chase these things when we first got together, but how was I supposed to tell the woman I loved all the vial things they did to me? I would die if the only thing she saw in me was what they have done to me, or forced me to do to them? so I lied. I lied to her. I lied to you and I sorry for that. I lied to Di. Now I am suffocating in my hidden shame." I cry franticly.

"Kioni, you are so much more than those acts… It isn't your shame to carry; you hear me? you were a child abused by a grown man. What they did to you was wrong on so many levels." Raven looked me in my eyes in hopes that I would see things from her point of view.

"Deshaun is going to hate me… If he ever finds out the truth he's gonna hate me… Raven I can't lose my son!" I shake my head side to side trying to fight what is on the verge of exposure.

Raven grabs me by my chin and turns my face to her. "Look at me! You are an exceptional mother and nothing from your past can ever change that. You and Chase have raised Deshaun to be an open-minded, intelligent, headstrong, and goal oriented young man. As far as telling him about his conception… once you have had time to think about things rationally, you will know what the best thing is to do… Kioni, I will be right here for you whenever you need me you know that… I love you!"

" For years I have kept things in order … Chase had even worked on her anger issues she hadn't raised her hand to me in almost two years… we were so happy… And now he's come and turned my world upside down again." I say.

"He?" Lines fill ravens forehead.

"One of my demons in the flesh; Zachery Steel Jr." Saying his name brings a thick silence between us because the steels stature is as well-known as the Trumps!

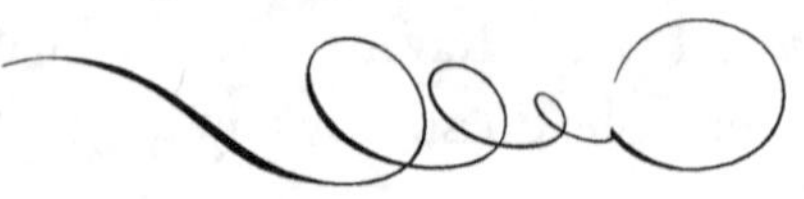

Cameron Carver

"Waiting on the manifestation of the sons of GOD." The female pastor spoke with conviction in her voice as she looked around the church from her pulpit.

"The only hope that the enemy has to paralyze your productivity is to cause you not to realize who you are intrinsically. Now, how can he then camouflage who you are intrinsically and internally. He does this by the external circumstance that grieves your heart… gradually convincing you that you have nothing left in you that is productive… but the devil is a liar!"

The pastor stretched out her arms as though she was pulling the congregation away from that misdirection.

"In fact when you begin to suspect that there is something inside of you, you become attractive to be around." The pastor looked at me and said.

"That is why we have to be careful who we have mentoring you. Because if they don't know who they are, they will kill you. Oh help me Jesus." The pastor moved her eyes around the church then centered them back on me and continued her sermon.

"We have too many Saul's in the church today. And the only reason Saul is trying to kill you is because he dies without discovering who he really is!"

My mother's eyes penetrate deeper than her words, she knows and pain floods my soul. I wish I could be who she wants me to be; the girl stuck on pink teddy bears, lost in a man's dream and stop being the same old me. I hold on to my bible and I pray facing east daily. And it hasn't changed who I love nor has it changed the way my mother loves me. In her mind there is nothing left to me if I don't lay with a man and eagerly reproduce his seed! I don't understand our lives or how hypocrisy reaps from her. She preaches when the church clearly looks down on a woman leading a flock. She told me that I was an African princess and the strength of a nation my whole life. Now that one of her sorority sisters and once closest friends confessed to her about our ongoing sexual relationship, she dismisses my identity and strips me of my queendom. I am loved only if I walk away from women and I become her belief. My mother reaches people every day, yet I am suffering from her emotional breach as a pastor and as a mother. I am barely breathing in this constricted relationship that has more distance in it than truth. And the more she preaches, the more my soul dies. I can't live my life through someone else's eyes, even when those eyes belong to her. So I put down the bible and I pick up a pen and let the ink bleed like blessings… It's funny how my words seem to reach the hearts of countless souls, yet fails to penetrate the one I long to reach the most.

Raven tilts her head back letting her head fall into the palm of my hand with ease. Her body lay partially across my lap and the chaise. I pour the warm water over her natural textured hair causing it to crinkle into curls. She softly moans and smiles with her eyes closed. She doesn't speak to me with words. Her body language tells me that she's enjoying what I'm doing to her. I place the picture on the stand then dip my hand into the bowl of oatmeal shampoo and let it drip at its own pace onto her damp hair. Then slowly I run my fingers through her hair causing it to lather and straighten to my touch. I massage her scalp from the lower bottom to her edges until I can feel the skin on my fingertips wrinkling and her body relax and give in to me from the other side of her silk kimono that pressed against my skin. I don't say a word either I let Maxwell's 'Silently' be my voice. I rinse her hair then wrap the plush towel around her head and help her sit up. Then I hold her soft hand in mine as she sits on the chaise inches from the one we were just on together. She licks her lips and blinks as though she could taste her thoughts. I pour her a glass of chilled Moscato and hand it to her. She waits for me to pour a glass for myself, then she leans over to me and kisses me with a kiss so sensual that it moves my soul. She is my temptress. She seduces me with her essence underneath the sky. It's been ten years of growth between us. I admire her strengths, build her weaknesses, and embrace her flaws the same as she does for me. I long her in every way. Her voice breaks through Silence as she tells me that she loves me. I reply to my wife… "I love you the same!" We both fill the night air from our screened in patio with laughter. Her smile captivates me. She is my completion, has been since the night I met her.

I was invited to a Halloween party by one of my coworkers. I walked through duplicate costumes of vampires with blood trailing the corners of their mouths, angels with sheer wings and halos, and devils with pointed tails and pitch folks and made my way to the bar. And there she sat with her light caramel complexion, big beautiful brown bedroom eyes, a sensual smile and her natural hair was in twists so small that they were damn near invisible and curly on the ends making her afro higher than the fake one I was wearing. The best part of me that I didn't even know I was missing. Raven steered at me and smiled because we were both members of the Black Panther Party. We were damn near identically dressed in all black with leather jackets that even matched. I was Huey P. Newton and she was Angela Davis.

Ramona Ndiaye

I am intrigued by the possibility, her intensity expressed in the few moments we shared at the gallery. Why am I going against the standards put on me by me, backed by time, proven by circumstances past that ended poorly. Bi-sexual, lesbian kryptonite seeped through her lips, yet mine still long to taste them. My days of playing with the fire that accompanies a woman that is not sure who or what she wants in her life are long gone... But her face keeps appearing in my mind, her voice replays in my ears, and no matter what I do to redirect my focus, Dianah Marshall consumes my thoughts. There is something in the confidence in her voice that compliments the truth in her hazel eyes when she looks at me. I love the way she looked at me like I was a woman plain and simple. See I have been around the world and indulged in the multitude of woman it has to offer. None of which viewed me without viewing my bank account, until Dianah Marshall. I've owned all the things that money can buy yet I long for the one thing in my life that can't be purchased and that's someone to love me... Growing up in Botswana, an only child of one of South Africa's wealthiest and prominent families, sincere people were hard to come by. When you have money, people respect your name, not you... Hell, they don't even try to know you. They just envy the money trail that you leave behind and the image that they see before them. And my family made sure that image was well maintained, from the preparatory schools, etiquette lessons, and charity events, leading up to my arranged Civil marriage to a distinguished man of power I never seen until the first day of the four day wedding ceremony but had been promised to since the age of five... Although the man's salt and pepper goatee possessed more gray then my fathers, the tide between the two families would ensure not only a history of strong offspring but form a political alliance that would be a force to be reckoned with.

I'm six hours into the age of sixteen and I'm being prepared for a man I don't want to be married to... and my mother's voice is colliding with my fear as she refreshes all the things I need to do to be a good wife from public appearances to satisfying him sexually. I've never been kissed, never had a boyfriend, or never fell in love the way the characters in the romance novels I read did. My mother finished talking nodded to the women in the room that gathered around enclosing us into the center of them. My mother began to undress me handing each piece of clothing to one of the women. I looked down at the burnt orange polish on my toes and nervously bit on my bottom lip as I stood nakedly. My mother held my face in her hands and kissed me then she turned and walked out of the room never looking back at me. The women led me to the claw foot bath tub sitting in the center of the bathroom that had been filled with warm milk which they placed me in. Then the oldest woman of the women began to wash me. She scrubbed my limbs like I hadn't bathed in weeks. When she was done cleaning my body all the women but two dried me off. Then they exited the room the same way my mother did never looking back. The two women that remained, their beauty was breathe taking. They didn't say a word they just rubbed perfume oil all over me where I stood. They moved their fingers soft and slowly up and down my body. I flinched as one of the beautiful woman's hand traced my breast and the others hand trailed my behind. The women smile at each other than at me they knew that their touch was arousing me. The women told me that what I was feeling was ok to feel... They told me that they were making my body ready for my husband... That this would make it easier to take... Each one took one of my hands and walked me over to the bed. Then one of the women touched my lips with her fingers then it happens I receive my fist kiss. She leans in and kisses me deep. And the other woman moves her tongue on the back of my neck and shoulders. I feel heat surge from my chest throughout my body. They lay me on the bed... They kiss and touch me in places that make me make sounds, that make me breathe faster, that make me tense then become relaxed, leaving me wet down there. Then they two exit the room without looking back. And within minutes my husband enters the room, the bed, and me... which he would do up until his assassination nine months later. Now here I stand miles and years away from that place, watching the slow but steady rain from my fifteenth floor Condo window in Miami tap then cover the shoulders of the pedestrians trying to reach some form of shelter, hailing taxi cabs and ducking under building doorways. The ring of my home phone brought life to my living room.

"Good morning Ms. Ndiaye." Dianah's voice sung a sweet melody in my ear.

"I was anticipating your call Ms. Marshall." I return her same formality totally confident that her calling me on my home line vs. my cell it would not be needed for long. I was fully aware of the reason for her call. I had the piece 'Divided' that she was so taken with delivered to her office located off of Rosewood Dr. this morning with the note: "I know your circumstance and I don't want to waste your time. In fact, I want to erase it and create new ways to log the days with you. Let me take you to dinner, lunch, breakfast, or all three. If you are not the restaurant type then let me cook for you. I don't want any miscommunication. I want to remove the distance that lies between the two of us getting to know each other. The painting isn't as beautiful without you in front of it… Enjoy!"

Soul Searching

Oh my god, tonight is long overdue. It's card night and everyone is gathered in the living room of my two bedroom townhouse. I made my chicken ravioli that everyone loves so much. So we are all trying to let our food settle as we partake in conversations and wine.

"Ivory, you put your foot in that!" Remy says as she pounds fists with me and sits in between Ebonee and Chase on the sectional.

"Ok now tell me about the dream you had that kept you up all night last week." Dianah ordered as she sat closely to Raven in anticipation of her response.

Raven sips her wine then begins to share her dream and we all turn our attention to hear the details of her dream as well.

"I had a nightmare that I was inside of an African turf war. And the turf members were recognized by different colors alone, being that their skin and features were all the same. I ran taking cover in a library, shielded by knowledge. Then I had my cover blown by an African American woman laughing and pointing at an African queen caring a waved basket on her head calm, peaceful, and posed through it all. So I began to run again with my heart pounding until I was called over by a brotha that began to teach me how to take a pill to become invisible when consumed. And to prove to me it works, he takes one and bumps into an elderly woman that was trying to teach the children gathered around her how to cut the elderly African warrior, from a distance to destroy him. She doesn't see him, So I watch the elderly woman as she betrays the children before they perfect the craft. And after spinning the lie to the closed eye African warrior who saw through her smiling eyes, He cut the tip of the elderly woman's tongue with her own hand sharpened blade, leaving her silenced and ridding the air of her trickery." Raven's eyes were full of tears like she was still trapped inside her nightmare.

Everyone sat in silence while Raven's words processes in our minds, then Cameron is the first to speak. "Raven and I sat up the remainder of that night trying to decipher the meaning of the dream and why it had the effect on he that it did…"

"I see why, the metaphors in the dream are uncanny… It feels like viewing the nightmare of today's reality through your eyes and the picture your dream painted is so clear that I feel the sadness that has formulated from the continued disconnection of our culture… So much so that you are trying to work it out in your subconscious!" Dianah said while she shook her head and took a sip of her drink.

"So what did you guys come up with after pondering over it?" Chase ask with intrigue.

"My interpretation of the dream was that the turf members where our brothers and sisters of color that were dropped off in different parts of the world and fight each other because they really think that their language makes them different when they are all of African descent. She used knowledge as a shield because most people don't educate themselves on their true history, so they would never look for her there. The African American woman laughing and pointing at an African queen caring a waved basket on her head is due to the ignorance of American born Africans that don't know or deny their own royal decent so they make fun of someone that does and is comfortable in their own skin. The brotha taking the pill to become invisible signifies people that use drugs to escape reality. As for the elderly woman, she is centuries of truth disguised and manipulated and she feeds that to the minds of children, and her lessons of deceit destroy them before they have a chance to mature. The elderly warrior symbolized wisdom, strength, and spiritual connection. So he saw her evil intent through her eyes… felt the depth of her ignorance that she spread through her smile laced words… So he turned the volatile attack that she had set in motion for him back on her, Karma or Destiny." Cameron said and sat back with a nonchalant look on her face like her translation of Raven's dream was one that any person of logic would have come to.

Wow, that's deep. The dream… the concepts… you guys are like the elderly warrior… you dream of peace. I love the strength that exudes from you strong women." Remy says as she rubs her chin with a smile.

I can't resist asking the question that Remy's reply just sparked in my mind so I place it on the floor for decision. "Open question… Are you a strong woman or a woman of strength?"

"I think that I would be a woman of strength for many reasons. Being the fourth generation descending from slavery, knowing that my great grandmother was left a house and land based on the beautiful job she did for the owners of the plantation, to my grandmother that was a care giver, that by title alone equates to low level respect given by others. To my mother having a good job as a nurse then down to me saying fuck it, I want be more than the nurturer pulling someone out of the depth of their death beds physically wearing my body down pushing me closer to mine. So I worked hard to not only attain my degrees, but my practice… Let alone being a black woman in America, which takes strength to be that woman…" Raven says as she let out a soft laugh.

"I feel like I am both because in every journey that I went into strong and fell weak in, somewhere I found the strength to pull through it and I still don't know where it come from." Ebonee says as though those moments' memories rush to the surface but she keeps them to herself.

"I feel that a strong woman and a woman of strength are one and the same. There is no strong without strength. When you went through those moments, your fear transcends into something else, strength, which in turn made you stronger." Chase says directly to Ebonee.

"I believe that we are all born with strong souls. We just have to learn how strong we are by mastering the use of our strengths." Kioni says giving raven and Dianah a look that only the three of them understand but the rest of us are used to seeing them share.

"I think that I am a strong woman because I have overcome many obstacles, myself being the biggest one and heartache in my life, caused by those who were supposed to love me most. And I am still here with love in my heart to give." I say and tears leave my eyes slowly, as I see the only person in the world I told I was an orphan already making her way over to me.

"Come here you big teddy bear!" Cameron says as she gave me a comforting hug that's as strong as our friendship and the secret she's kept about me for years.

Remy Gamble

She opens the door a few seconds after my three tap knock on it.

"Hey Daddy," Thick Mrs. answers the door with nothing but her T-shirt and panties on. I great her with a smile, lick my lips, and let my ego rise to the occasion as I walk through the door and into her living room.

"Damn Ma, I thought you was playin with a Nigga's head saying you was ready." I admit the doubt I had about her decision to take this step.

"Does this look like I'm playing?" She walks over, runs her fingers through the root of my freshly re-twisted dreads, shucks my bottom lip into her mouth, runs her hand down the front of my pants, then steps away with a confident smile as she close and locks the door. By the time she turns around I'm already on her. I run my fingers up her thick thighs, play with the pink lace that trims the black of her panties a perfect symbol of her girly yet dark side. I grip her hair pulling it away from her neck before I suck on it firmly. Thick Mrs. let out a moan, grips the back of my head and assist me with having my way with her as we move franticly through the living room, knocking over any and everything in our path as we make our way to the couch. I bent her over the back of the coach, prop her right leg on top of it. I pulse long enough to get a condom out of its wrapper and on to my shit before I pull her panties to the side and slid into her.

"Ha" she moans, inhales, and grabs the couch like she is receiving what her body has been missing and although I know this is the wrong thing to do, I don't stop.

"Yeah, I knew you had a fat ass pussy… pop that wet shit on my dick."

"Oh yeah Daddy, fuck me. Fuck me hard." She says as she bounces against my hard.

I grip her shoulders and thrust myself deep inside her. The sound of her ass smacking against my dick makes me want to fuck her more. So I smack her on her ass. I make her squeal. I make her pussy wetter.

"You like the way I put it on you, don't you…" I say confidently.

"Yeah, Daddy, yeah, You been working long and hard to get in this pussy , now fuck me like you said you would… That's right like that… yeah, handle this pussy make it yours , Daddy" she says as she looks back at me, grunts like she is fighting the fact that I'm not her Mrs.. She regains her rhythm, nibbles on my finger, and then sucks it into her mouth deep sending a clear message of how good she can work her mouth on my shit. Which I'm sure she'll be doing just that by the end of the night.

"Is this pussy good to you? Do you like the way I ride, daddy?" she ask me as she moves her hips in a tick tock motion.

I didn't answer her with words. I grab her ponytail, wrapping it around the center of my hand, and make her bend and I go all in. I works the hell out of that pussy, until she comes hard, then our bodies fall unto the couch. Our breathing is short and heavy. We look at each other both of our faces are covered with sweat.

"Did you cum?" she ask breaking the silence as she slides next to me, now positioned the correct way on the couch.

"Naw, but I'm about to!" I say as I guide her head down in my lap. I watch my little man disappear into her mouth and reappear. Thick Mrs. works her mouth like a pro as she runs the tip of her fingernails along my fat outer lips, causing my shit to get rock hard under sticks her sticky finger in my ass.

"What the fuck… Shit… Ah…" I want to get mad at her putting her finger in my ass but honestly… The stimulation of her finger in my ass is bringing me to my point. She looks at me, grips my dick and pulls it up out of her way,then she takes my rock hard clit into her mouth sucking hard like I was shooting into her mouth and she was drinking every drop, until I collapse in her mouth and on her hand. She eases out of my ass and let my shit drop out of her mouth and sat back on the couch, smells her fingers, then licks them.

"Damn!" I look at her shining in the aftermath of what we have done. There is no regret that I can see, and none that I will show to her.

"Fuck, I'm hungry." She says as she sat up.

"Hungry ain't the word."

The song, "There goes my baby…" interrupts our moment causing her face to change and her body to stiffen beside me before she gets up and walks out of the room to answers her cell phone. I stand up and readjust my clothes. I replace all the things that we knocked over in my friend's home, while we went at it. Then I push the button on the air freshener mounted on the wall a few times to get the smell of pussy out of the air.

Thick Mrs. comes out dressed with her bag in hand, turning out the lights as she approaches me.

"Thanks for straightening up." She says with a halfhearted smile.

"No problem Ma, everything alright?" I question as she looks at me with different eyes.

"Yeah, you said you were hungry… let's get you something to eat."

"You gonna feed a nigga too? That's what's up." I say playfully rubbing my stomach.

"I got you. You know you're my boo… So anywhere you want to eat is fine, but we have to eat there, ok?"

"That's straight." I say looking in her eyes and there it was, what I didn't want to see, but was glad she felt just a little bit, the look of regret. She take one more glance around the living room to make sure all was in place as she holds the air freshener down to refill the room with a pleasant scent, then turns out the light, locks up, and exits with me.

Kioni Wils

I stand over the blood stained mattress and soiled white sheets in the center of the backyard that I dragged from our bedroom. I go back inside the house and snatch off all the framed pictures of Chase and me that cover the living room walls and place them in the center of the mattress. I gather whatever gifts of love that Chase brought me over the years that I can make out through my tears and add them to all the past and present pain that seems to be the sum of my life and I drench them with lighter fluid. I take out a long steam match that I normally would use to light the grill and I slide its tip along the rugged side of its box and toss it. I feel the heat of the fire next to my flesh as the symbols of all my painful memories and broken promises melt and wither in the flames. I glare into the flame and watch it quickly become an inferno. And I wonder if I were to through my battered and broken body into the fire, if it would become purified by the flames. I wonder if then they would love me… truly love me.

"Ma'am, are you okay? Is there anyone else inside the house?" I hear the deep voice of the fireman asking me over and over while he practically carries me to a corner of the yard that was away from the growing hazard I created.

"No… No one else is here." I answer as I wipe away the tears from my eyes.

"I need more hose!" A firefighter yells as he works to put out the raging inferno.

I'm so engulfed in my emotions that I didn't hear the loud sirens that are now blaring all around me or even notice that the fire has traveled beyond the center of the yard where I started it at to over half of the yard, torching everything in its path including part of the neighbors' mango tree, and was inches from reaching my house.

"Kioni, are you ok? Where is Deshaun? Baby what happened? Where is Deshaun?" Chase yells out as she runs through the yard towards me then wraps her arms around me before I can tell her that Deshaun and I are fine physically…That I dropped Deshaun at his friend's house for the weekend before I came home and tried to gather every picture of us together and gift that she has ever given me and set it ablaze.

"James, we are done here. It's safe to enter your premises now." the firefighter called out Chase's last name in acknowledgement of her position as one of BSO finest detective
s.
"Thank you!" Chase replies with gratitude barely taking her eyes away from me.

"Let me make you aware that what you did is not only dangerous but it's considered arson in the state of Florida? Given your profession I know that you know you could have lost your life, not just your home. " The Captain of the firefighters looks me in my eyes that I am sure are red and swollen by now.His voice is stern with a hint of compaction as he points out the severity of my actions and the tragedies that could have happen if they hadn't reached me in time.

"I didn't think that it would get out of hand." I say softly.

"People never do." He says as he hands me a written warning about proper disposal of trash and turns to walk away. Chase lets me go to walk him back to his truck to do some damage control I'm sure.

"It won't happen again. I assure you!" Chase says as she looks back at me sternly then back to the captain just before they exit the back yard.

"Do you know how this makes me look or even worse, what the fuck this could do if this got back to my precinct?" Chase says in an aggravated tone as she returns to find me in the same spot she had left me in.

I look up to my lover as she looks down at me. I replay the expression she had on her face as she ran over and held me so tight in her arms, I replay how quickly she came to save me in my mind. Then I touch the badge that hangs on her waste and I ask her…

"What do I have to do… what do I have to do to make you love me?" I search her eyes for truth.

"I do love you." Her mouth speaks what her emotions showed me moments ago.

"What do I say when you hit me?" I ask as soon as she answers my first question.

"Is that what this is about? Let's go inside!" she says as she pulls me by my arm trying to guide me into the house, but I pull away from her.

"No, no more hiding for either one of us. We do this here, now, or we don't do this at all… What do I say, Chase?" I demand a reply firmly with my eyes.

"Do what, Kioni? talk about you… about you leaving me… Talk about you taking my son, the son you said was our son away from me… Talk about losing the only things that are good in me… I don't' want to talk about that!" Chase looks at me with both intolerance and defeat in her watered eyes.

"What do I say, Chase?" I scream.

"You tell me that you love me!" she yells.

"I tell you that because I do love you. I love you with all that I am!" my words are filled with so much truth that hurts.

"If you love me then why were you leaving me? We were doing well or at least I thought we were. We hadn't fought in damn near two years. Yet you were packing up and about to walk out my life without saying a word to me." She says as a tear rolls down her face.

"Chase, my love, It wasn't you that I was running away from." I softly touch my lovers face and begin to tell her what I never should have kept from her in the first place.

"I was thirteen when my mother's husband brought Zachary Steele Jr. into my room and closed the door behind him for the first time. It was Zeke's sixteenth birthday. That's what everyone called him except his father, Zachary Steele Sr." I pause but I don't look at Chase right now in fear that I won't say what I have held in for far too long.

"Today you become a man." He said then told us to get undressed. My step brother and playmate at times looked at my naked body as he climbed on top me, and did as he was told. Our eyes connected through tears and for a few moments, I was not alone in my hidden shame. Zeke moved nervously inside me and it didn't take long for him to shake and get off of me. He looked back at me lying there crying, then he grabbed his pants and ran out of the room, leaving the door open. I thought that my mother's husband would follow him out, but he didn't. He just closed and locked the door. Then he turned around and started taking off his clothes, revealing to me for the first time what had been the cause of my pain many times before."

"Baby…" Chase calls out to me as she reaches out to comfort me. But I hold out my hand asking her to stay where she is and let me say what I must… and she does.

"You like feeling him inside of you, don't you?" He asked me but I didn't know what to say to him, so I didn't say anything. I just held on to the cover as tight as I could. I knew by the look in his eyes that I had done something wrong and he was angry with me. He rushed over to the bed and snatched the sheet from my grasp, and took its place in between my legs. I tried… I tried to fight him, but I was so small compared to him." I glance at Chase, and see the tears trailing her face as hard as they are from mine but I go on.

"Ouch," I yelled as he roughly made entry into my body. He was enraged by his own actions and I was about to feel what I know now to be the wrath of his jealousy.

"This pussy … You… Will always belong to me!" he said in my ear as he violated my womb of thirteen years.

"Aw, stop. Please don't." I screamed. He didn't cover my mouth or make offers to buy me things to quiet me up like he usually did. So I screamed as loud as I could. I screamed for my mother. I screamed for her to come and help me. I screamed for her to make him stop hurting me. I screamed over and over but she never came. I knew she was home.. That she could hear my cries, but she never came. I guess the pain he was causing me was a small price to pay for the wealth and status that she gained by being Mrs. Zachary Steele. I screamed when he grabbed my legs. I screamed when he forced them farther apart. I screamed when he pushed himself inside of me and shook. I screamed until he was done shaking inside me but he didn't leave my bed that night. Neither did the rest of the innocence I didn't know I had left neither did my voice." Chase takes my hands into hers without saying a word and lets me finish.

"My mother's husband would force Zeke and me to have sex in front of him. Then do unspeakable things to me afterwards, until Zeke went to college. I'm so sorry…There is no Hatethem… I've only been with two men my whole life." I look at my lover. She let go of my hands and hold her chest over her heart and ask through strained words…

"Who's Deshaun's father?"

"It could be either one." My answer is as hard for me to say as it is for my lover to hear.

Chase falls to her knees in the saturated grass and lets out a silent scream that echoes through my soul as she begins to rock with pain. I drop down beside her and grab her face.

"Baby… I'm so sorry… I never meant to lie to you but I couldn't tell you the truth about Deshaun's' father without telling you about the horrible things I had been forced to endure … I was too ashamed to tell you… to afraid that you wouldn't love me if you knew… that you couldn't… love… someone as dirty as me!" I confess through my tears and shame.

"Kioni, I love you and Deshaun…What you just told me doesn't change that.. And for anytime I have ever made you feel otherwise I apologize … hurting you in any way was never my intent… Baby I love you and I've never wanted anything more than I want you and my son in my life forever!" Chase takes my hands into hers and kisses them over and over again.

"I want to be…" I say softly as I look at her and tense up a little not knowing how she is going to take the last thing that I have to tell her in order to lay all my fears in the palm of her hands completely.

"Zeke was at Deshaun's game. I don't know how he found us and until that moment, I didn't even think that he knew I was pregnant let alone that he had ever laid eyes on Deshaun. To my knowledge my mother was the only one that saw him. My mother fell silent and her skin went pale when she did… she looked at Deshaun's face then she looked at me with tears in her eyes then turned and hurried out the hospital room… Three days later she came back to pick us up and told me that she and her husband planned on adopt and raise my baby as their own, a Steele… I couldn't stop him from hurting me but I would die before I let him take my baby from me… So I snuck pass my mother and out of the hospital with Deshaun while she discussed the procedures of adoption with a nurse."

"He was at the game? Why didn't you tell me?" She ask me with a hint of confusion in her face.

"Yes… he was at the game sitting in the bleachers across from us and I panicked. Thoughts started running through my head… like if he knows who Deshaun is… where his private school is… then he knows where he lives… were we live. So I just thought about getting as far away as I could… then you did what you did to me!" My words remind my lover of her wrong doing and make her face her own demons, as I'm forced to face mine.

"Oh my God! what have I done? Oh God, please forgive me!" Chase cried out in agony as she grabs her stomach.

Cameron Carver

When Raven smiles I want to kiss the curves that form it. When she laughs, I want to dive into the sound and examine the vibration. When she sleeps, I want to be in her dreams. When I touch her body I want to travel her soul. I don't know why, but the more she gives to me, the more I want from her. Each time I look at her I see her in a new light. Her love is like oxygen and without it I fail to exist. I have consumed her in every way and I feel like there is so many more ways to achieve the same consumption. I am obsessed with her and I am her obsession. At times I want to imprison her inside my heart so she truly knows that she is the cause of each beat it takes. The love I have for my wife is one that has no definition or comparison. Yet I have been told by the lovers of broken relationships that once over flowed with happy days and sleepless nights that my desire for Raven will fade. It's been a decade and the Jones we have for one another is still going strong. And my desire has transformed into invite because I don't control her love, I welcome it as it welcomes me, intensively which causes me to scrutinize my actions, intentions, and thoughts.

What do you do when your mind tells you that you don't need to use additives in the bed room? But your soul craves the feeling you get when you do. The feeling of knowing that you have made love to her completely. I know that a woman can be satisfied with just fingers, tongues, lips, and skin… Hell, I'm one of them yet I'm such a walking contradiction to my own concepts. I'm shaking my head at myself, but I am who I am. I've always wanted to be that person on the other end of pleasure; the pleasure giver to woman, from tracing her eyebrows with my lips to following the lines that make up the curves in her toes with my tongue. I've always wanted to be the one that makes a woman inhale air and her desire at the same time, then lose her breath because her desire and need to be desired is met. Then push her to her limits that cause her to create new ones to break. I am a lover of women completed by one. Just saying that makes my blood rush through my body, then slowly seep into the tissue that lays beneath my skin keeping it alive. And for the most part I know that my lover is fine with that part of me. But I know that her love for women is as strong as my love for them.

I can tell by the look in her eyes, the way her breathing is getting shallow as she softly runs her face along my cheek letting the heated breath from her nostrils brush my ear lobe, the way she's sucking my tongue into her mouth like it belongs to her and it does, the way she's caressing my breast, the way she's grabbing the meat of my inner thigh with intensity tells me she wants me… she wants me to give in to her the way that she gives herself to me, willingly. Raven has her tomboy on and wants to take me for a ride. Her soft lips plead with me with each kiss. The longing of a woman that loves woman steers her desire and causes her to open my legs with hers. She kisses me deep as she breaks through the lips between my thighs. Her moan tells me that her huger is great but I don't give her what she longs. I remove her hand with my own. She doesn't fight me about it physically. She sucks her teeth and verbalizes her disappointment with my refusal.

"This shit is so unfair." she says as she looks down at me from a push up position over me.

"I'm sorry" I apologizes with a hint of embarrassment in my voice because I want to please her in every way but this one I just can't seem to master. I try, lord knows I have tried and succeeded a few times over the ten years we have been together but tonight just isn't one of them.

"Don't be sorry… let me have what's mine!" she orders kissing and sucking on my neck. Then she runs her finger over my clit.

"Boobie!" I call out to my lover in a tone that asks her not to proceed.

"Buddha! Come on… it's so wet." She looks at me with the same intent in mind.

"I'll use a lot of lube and be gentle so you can get used to it." She says as she leans over to retrieve the lube and prepare her pleasure.

"Ooh…" I quietly moan and my body tenses as she begins to satisfy her desire.

"Relax… baby it will feel better once its inside. She says as she continues to work the tip in with gentle but needed force.

I close my eyes bit down on my bottom lip and try harder to give her what she craves from me. My world spins and my pulse throbs as she enters me deep. I try to calm my nerves before they transform into reserve and make me disappoint her again. I meditate to the sound of her breath, I focus on her smile, I try and inhale the scent of her skin until I can taste her flavor on my tongue and I swallow. I endure a few more pumps before I give up.

"Ah!" I inhale. "Ouch! Wait… I can't take it bay… please…" I try to keep her from going any deeper by scooting up but she fallows my lead till my head hits the head board.

"You look so sexy… I love … being inside of you." She kisses my neck in between her words.

"Baby… It hurts … I'm… too tight!" I say as I push the palms of my hands against her shoulders.

"You wouldn't be if you let me fuck you more often! It's been well over two years since you let me have some." She said as she eases out of me in a vexed tone.

"Bay… it's only been a few days since you had some!" My eyes remind her of her Ndia.

"That's not that same fucking thing and you know it… she's not you" she snaps and walks to the bathroom to wash away the evidence of her disappointment. Raven comes back to where I lay and does the same to the traces between my legs without saying a word to me then returns to the bathroom.

I wipe away the tears from my eyes as quickly as they fall. I am not the crying type so I definitely don't want her to see my liquid pain. My throat burns and my heart aches from her words, sometimes I feel so inadequate. I wish that I could take back the vow of honesty that we made to each other when we first met. I wish I could suck up the pain I feel when she is inside me and allow her to drive until the lines in this road fade and put her to sleep.

"I'm sorry I shouldn't have said that to you!" Raven says as she sat on the bed beside me and touches my face. Her eyes are as red as I imagine mine to be in this moment. She has been crying.

"We can try again… I think I'll be ok now." I say with a hint of a smile. I want to fulfill her need for me even if it kills me doing so.

"I wouldn't enjoy it knowing that I'm hurting you!" she says as she touches my face.

I look at my wife and remember how well she knows me and can't stop my tears from falling into her hands.

"Cameron, baby… I love you… I know your strength and I love your dominance… you know that… but I love and need your femininity too!" she kisses the corners of my eyes, my cheeks, then my lips letting our tears mix together before she climbs in bed in front of me. She presses her hips against my warmth, places my hand in hers pulling my arm over her waist and holding on to me until she falls asleep.

Ebonee Price

I inhale your scent while I hold on to the back of your navy blue wife beater as you move your head and tongue in between my legs. Each lick making my pussy purr louder and my words shorter. My body trembles from satisfaction. Your precision in location, pressure, tempo, and moister reminds me how well you know my body… how well you know what I like… how well you know what I need to reach my point. If only you were that precise out of the bedroom. I don't even know why I'm letting you do this to me right now. I am so over you and your broken promises to love me. I know you are still my lover but that's only by title. I love you but I am no longer in love with you. I don't even feel guilty for feeling this way anymore. I have pleaded with you for months to love me… to show me this affection without the sex… to show me that you want me. Show me that you need me the way that I once needed you.

"Ah… yeah… baby… just like that… It feels so good…" Ivory brings me out of my mind from the pleasure she is giving me.

"You wanna cum in my mouth don't you?" She asks in her usual cocky tone.

"Hell yes… I want to cum so… fucking hard… baby… make me cum… oh God … baby make me … cum!"

She picks up the paste of her tongue sucking on my clit to match the speed of the two fingers she's vibrating inside of me.

"Oh fuck… yeah… I'm about to… fucking… shit…" I buck my hips hard on her fingers and cover them with my juice. She quickly removes them and sticks her tongue in deep to taste my flavor. That makes me shake, twitch, and fight to catch my breath. I feel her hands rubbing and touching me as she makes her way up my body and to my face.

"Kiss me and lick your pussy juice off my lips."

"No baby" I turn my face away from Ivory's. It's one of the things I use to enjoy doing but I no longer want to share myself with her like that.

"No? I'm not asking… lick your fucking pussy juice off my lips!" she grabs me by my hair and makes me look at her. But I still don't kiss her. She pulls harder and the pains enough to make me take her top lip into my mouth and take in my sweetness. My body is in her arms but my mind is filled with thoughts of someone else. I feel Ivory reach for the head of her strap.

"Bay take it from the back." Ivory looks at me like she wants to say something but she doesn't. She knows if she says the wrong thing it will all come to an end. She just rises up and walks to the side of the bed. I get on my knees and no sooner than I do she pushes my head into the pillows and arches my ass higher.

"Is this what you want" she asked me in my ear as she mounts me. I cover her mouth.

"Shut up and fuck me"

I don't want to hear her voice I don't want to feel her touch. All that I have longed for from Ivory has died… this is the only place she wants my love… it only seems fitting that this is where I take it away from her once and for all.

She rams her ten inch in me and I don't make a sound. I don't give her what she feeds off of. I don't tell her how good she feels. I don't tell her how rough she's handling her pussy. I don't stroke her ego. I just through myself into her taking all she has to give. I demand her to work harder to give me more. I made her catch up to my orgasms and then leave her behind again. Then when I have my fill of Ivory I bring her to the beginning of a climax and remove her from inside me.

"What the fuck?" She stands there looking like she lost her best friend.

"Take that off and lay on the bed!" My voice is cold and direct.

She takes off her strap as she watches me put on mine. I grab the water base lube and lather it up. Tonight there won't be any licking or persuasion from my end.

"Open your legs" I order and she does what I tell her to. I enter her dripping secrete. She inhales and I take it all in and add it to my memory... her facial expression... her breathing... the way she grips the sheets... moves her hips...

"Mm mm…. Ah… baby" Ivory's moans starts to grow in sound.

I cup her breast in my hands. I suck her thick pink nipples into my mouth one at a time until her flush turns to red. I work my ass between her thighs and I feel her wetness increase.

"Ooh yeah… have me the way you want me."

Have you the way I want you. I want her like this outside of this got damn room. Off of this bed. Like this in the mild of our friends. Her words made me insane. I grab her by her hair, bit into her neck and began to fuck her without mercy.

"Ooh…"

She turns her head from side to side like she is fighting off each wave of pleasurable pain I am delivering. I make her want me to stop then need me to continue at the same time. I make her fall in love with my sex game as deeply as I fell in love with her promises. I make her fall for me so many times that her body won't stop shaking underneath me.

"I love you!" Ivory declares through shallow breaths.

I examine her face understand her emotion in the after math of pleasure because I have been there too many times to count. So I am not moved by her use of words. I no longer desire her or her love. I pull out of her without caution and head for the shower.

"What the fuck is this?" Ivory screamed over the running water as she snatch the rust color shower curtain open with one hand and holding a black and white Bareback in the other.

"It's a condom." I reply as if I don't see the anger in her face.

"I know what the fuck it is! I want to know how the fuck it got in my house, let alone under my fucking couch!"

"I don't know… We don't use them honey!" I answer nonchalantly.

"Are you fucking someone else Ebonee?" she ask me with tears in her eye.

"Who would want an immature bitch like me?" I look at Ivory standing there with her tidies hanging holding the fucking Bareback in the air like it was the item she brought to class for show and tell. I watch the tears leave her eyes and think to myself how humorous the sight of her jealousy is. I cut my eyes at her then I close the shower curtain and continue to wash away her sent that was as strong as my actions.

Chase James

"**C**an a person change?" I ask sitting upright transferring perspiration from one palm to the other, afraid of what Nina Miles's response would be. Dr. Nina Miles, the psychiatrist Cameron highly recommended to me after Raven assured her that Mrs. Miles was more than a qualified psychiatrist but a trusted colleague and Raven is certain she can help me.

"We are all born with choice so that gives us all the ability to change, what you have to determine is what type of impact you want your actions to have while you do." Her voice is soft and clear. It doesn't contain any condemnation or judgment. Nor does her chestnut eyes contradict her voice as they look at me with warmth.

"I mean really change… change from their soul… not just their mental state… because anyone can look at something with disgust and still continue to look at it… still commit the very acts that they find grotesque! " I state and lower my head, too ashamed of the things I have done, ashamed of the thing I have become, to let my eyes met hers in this moment.

"What acts are those?"

"I… I hit her." My body tenses as I hear my own words.

"Her who?" She sits up a little in her chair.

"Kioni, my partner… I hit her!" I saying Kioni's name makes a wave of heat rush through my body.

"Was that an isolated incident?" Mrs. Miles questions in a soft tone looking me straight in my eyes certain that she would find the truth there.

"No."

"How many times has it occurred?" She watches me while jotting notes on her tablet.

"I hit Kioni once after stopping for a nearly two years, before that I don't know how many times I hit her… too many…. I always hated myself afterwards… I would always vow to make each time the last time… every time!" I turn and focus on the raindrops that have begun to tap on the window to the right of me. I notice how it is positioned right in front of the dark brown chaises that I opted not to sit on when I entered the room minutes earlier.

"So why hasn't it been?" She ask me directly in a firm tone.

"I don't know… It's not a high to hit her." I turn away from the rain and look back at her.

"What do you feel when you hit her?"

"It's quite the opposite. Because she becomes the me that the monster I become keeps me from being." I answer her with complete honesty surprising myself.

"I see… and kind of you would that be?"

"A weaker… frightened… one!" I shift my body.

"Chase, do you feel that the only way a person can exist is to function as an abuser or as a victim of abuse?" She lays her pen down and waits for reply.

"Yes… yet both abuser an victim are victims of some form." I reply adamantly.

"Do you feel that you are a victim?"

Her question catches me off guard and reaches the core of me. I'm silent for a few minutes before I give my painful reply.

"Not in this situation… I'm definitely not a victim in this situation… But I never knew…" Tears streamed my face as the pain explodes inside my chest, sending ripples of agony through my soul once again. How could I have taken what Kioni has always given to me freely? I have to release my skeletons completely and expose my darkest deed.

"What didn't you know?" Mrs. Miles ask with concern now in her voice as she walks to the front of her desk that she allows her lower coke bottle shaped body to lean on. All the while getting closer to me but giving me space at the same time.

"I never would have taken her that way… I just wanted to make her feel my need for her…I wanted to make her feel good… good enough to stay with me… I didn't know… I swear… I didn't know… Deshaun is my son. He's been since he was eight… I would die for them both with no hesitation… They are all that's good in me…" I tell her my soul's truth with pain in my heart, burn in my chest, and nausea in my throat. "I didn't know that Kioni had been molested and Deshaun was a product of her molestation… I swear… I didn't know… I'm so ashamed and disgusted with myself!" I rock as the tears begin to fall.

"You can't hold the shame and disgust you feel inside you in forever." Mrs. Miles advise as she touches my hand with hers and looks at me with tender eyes.

"How do I make the image of what I have done fade from my mind? How do I make the pain that I have caused Kioni fade from hers? What I did… no matter how many times I say I'm sorry it won't erase the things that I've done. I can't take back my wrongs… I can't take back my wrongs!" I spoke through tears and regret.

Mrs. Miles says six words that are destine to bring change to my life… "This is where the healing starts!"

And I begin to cry harder than I have cried in years.

Raven Winters-Carver

I watch Cameron enter N'dia slow and deep. I watch her grab a hold to Cameron's arms as if they are life preservers, keeping her afloat. I watch N'dia fight to keep her emotional tie estranged from my lover. I'm not quite sure if it is out of respect for me as a woman, us as a couple, or to guard herself from the state of vulnerability. At any rate, I know it was a battle she will not win, it isn't her fault. I know exactly what she's feeling right now because I too lost that battle time and time again.

"Ooh… my…God" she lets out as Cameron circles inside her valley slowly. Cameron's rhythm is unrushed, grounded by the desire to introduce Ndia to ecstasy like no one before her has done.

"Shit…" Cameron moans, looks me in my eyes, grips N'dia breasts and waits, waits for me to tell her how I want her to make Ndia feel. If I deem N'dia's loyalty worthy of the pleasure Cameron is capable of delivering or the torture that always lies beneath the smirk in Cameron's smile. I lean in over N'dia's head, kiss on her on the right side of her neck, as Cameron sucks on her left.

"Mmm…" N'dia lets out as she runs her hand through my hair and bites me on my shoulders.

"Does she feel good inside you?" I ask my feminine lover in her ear.

"Yes…. Ooh God… yes…" she replies softly, then reaches down to my stomach, over my shaven area and enters my wet sweetness, takes it out then licks me off of her fingers.

"You taste so good." She says as she reenters me, as though time is of the essence. This time she holds my leg with her left hand and finger fucks me with her right.

"Hum…." I move my body on her hand and Cameron kisses me while she is still slow stroking our lover. N'dia and I are composing of melody of moans and I give Cameron the ok to please us both. Cameron kisses N'dia long and intensely. Moves her ass at a medium tempo, easing out then back in just enough to caress Ndia's first G-spot. Cameron brings N'dia to her point in less than 5 minutes of her change in rhythm but eases back just before N'dia releases, making her moans increase, making her body shake, making her plead to cum, but Cameron denies her. Cameron is making Ndia dig into her skin, claw her back, ass, and legs. Cameron is making N'dia explore the waves of eroticism.

"Baby let me taste you." N'dia says to me through stagnant breaths.

"Humph, don't play with it if I give it to you. You better swallow every drop." I laugh as I forewarn her as she begins. N'dia smacks me on my left ass cheek then pulls me onto her long and thick tongue that meets my heated wet with urgency.

"Fuck yeah, eat my pussy." I say grabbing my nipples and squeezing them. N'dia is good, really good with her tongue. She's sucking me from the inside, licking my lips and taking my clit into her mouth firmly. Then back to tongue fucking me, she's doing this to me over and again, causing me to brace myself on the wall with one hand and the bed with the other. She's sucking and I am grinding. I can fell the wetness running down my walls and I cum in her mouth. She licks me dry till I shake and cum again, and shake.

"Ok… ok… I can't take it anymore… too…. Sensitive right now."

She lets me lose from her grip and I crawl to the side of them. Jerk and shake a few more times as I catch my breath. Cameron looks at me, knows that I am pleased, so she focuses on her. Cameron opens

N'dia legs wider, strokes her deeper and harder than before. Cameron makes her moan out loud, makes her grip the sheets, makes her bite her fingers. Cameron sucks on N'dia's neck, her ears, then her breasts. Pulls out, goes deep, and then strokes her in circles. N'dia shakes, cries out that she's gonna cum. Pleads for Cameron to let her fucking cum and Cameron does. Cameron makes her cum slow and hard, makes her feel each trickle that trails her inner walls. N'dia holds on to Cameron, kisses her, and looks Cameron in her eyes as she shakes underneath her. Then Cameron hits N'dia's second G-spot located in the back at the top, that we discovered within the first month of our relationship becoming sexual and she stops breathing… doesn't know whether to push away or hold on… before she can decide Cameron hits it harder and N'dia is cumming without warning. N'dia squeals, and then shakes.

"Ooh my God…. Shit… ooh….fuck…." Cameron is hitting her third G-spot at the bottom left. N'dia's screaming, laughing, biting, and scratching, as she cums in a wave of powerful multiples. Then Cameron slows down her intensity, letting N'dia breathe a little before she pulls out easy. N'dia shakes, mumbles…. Then looks at me and starts to cry.

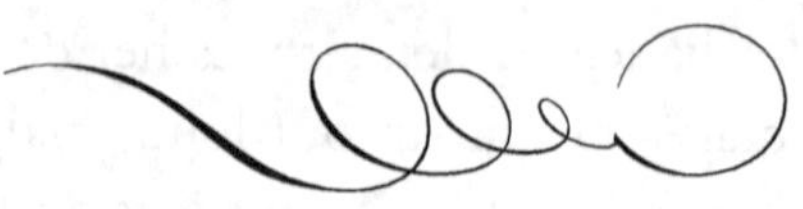

Dianah Marshall

I find myself staring into Ramona's eyes examining the amount of moisture that remains on her lips as she sips sparkling champagne from her flute. She looks around her elegant space that is the size of four luxurious duplex penthouses and that now has dramatic floor-to-ceiling glass walls and a phenomenal view towards the ocean that adds to the sophisticated design. And newly customized kitchen combined with top-of-the-line appliances and heated Italian wood floors. I would like to say that it was a job that I completed by myself, but honestly Ramona was here almost every other day. I know it wasn't because she didn't have any place else to relax seeing that she had taken up residency at the Loews on Collins Avenue while her place was being remodeled, it was her need to be close to me in any way possible… as she put it when she offered me the opportunity. Ramona made it very clear that she would still like more from me then a working relationship but she is willing to take any interaction that she can have with me rather than none at all. By the end of dinner, I allow Ramona to talk me into remodeling a home on the beach that she recently purchased for one of her out of state friends, that fell in love with Miami a few years ago when she first came to the states as a business associate. So Ramona feels the three bedroom two bathroom overlooking the water, would be the perfect present for her friends twenty-fifth anniversary since she makes it a point to return every. A little part of me can't help but wonder if this friend of hers is really someone she's been intimate with or interested in. Not that I have any right to be jealous about who she is or isn't seeing when I turned down the position. I think she feels my reserve because she hands me a card with a name and number on it that belongs to her friend's lover. Ramona tells me that I will be dealing solely with her friend's lover on this project, but whatever she desires to have done to the place I have the okay to fulfill, although she will be the one footing the bill. I smile, place the number on the table closest to me, and continued to admire my own work.

Ever since the completion of the beach house, the phones in my office have been ringing off the hook. A lot of the calls are form the friends and associates that were in attendance at the anniversary party and others are calling because someone they know is highly impressed with the job my team and I have done to the beach house. I'm definitely not complaining about the increased workload I'm facing, but based off of the five voice mails and ten text messages from Vance within the hour it took me to shower and get dressed, tells me that he is clearly above his level of tolerance with my absence.

"Where the hell are you?" Vance snaps after he picks up in the middle of the first ring.

"Excuse me?" I cut my eyes at my IPhone .

"You were supposed to be here an hour and a half ago!" I can see his face through his voice as though I was standing in front of him. His right eyebrow is arched and his lips are turned up.

"Calm down, I'm leaving my house now…" I say pulling out of the driveway.

"You're leaving now?! You know what …don't even brother!" I hear what seems to be him slamming the chair against the table as he walks away from it.

"Baby don't be dramatic… there is still plenty of time for us to get together and enjoy one another."

"I'm sick and tired of having late dinners with you, Dianah… that's why I made reservations." His breathing sounds like heavy wind blowing.

"I understand that! And I'm trying to get things together so that you don't have to for much longer." I inhale silently.

He pauses and I hear the beep of the restaurant door opening and closing, then he continues his rant.

"You have been putting me on the back burner for far too long. It's like a new habit of yours, along with your apologies through text messages and I don't like it. I will no longer tolerate your behavior or lack of intimacy!" His voice is laced with distain.

The way he says those last words strikes something inside of me.
"No longer tolerate?!" I take a deep breath. "I understand your frustration with me right now but watch your tone!" I fight hard to keep my temper inline.

"Watch my tone... I'll watch my tone with you when you remember that I am your fucking man... when you remember that I need more than a got damn hour lunch with you, Dianah... Or when you remember that I want to feel more then cold air on the empty side of my bed where you are supposed to be... When you remember that I desire to share a life with you not just spared damn moments!"

"I don't need a fucking reminder of who you are, Vance...you know that things have picked up and I have a full work load! I would think that you would support me and have a little more understanding." I say as I tighten the grip I have on the steering wheel.

"Yeah and you just made it clear on where I fit in!"

"Those are your words not mine... I don't understand why we have to go through this in the first place. I've always had your back in whatever you did... You know what... fuck it! I said that I'm sorry for running late. I don't know what else you want from me." I rub my temples while I wait for the light to turn green and my stress level mounts.

"Are you seeing someone else?" He ask like he knows what the answer to his question is before he asked it.

"What? Where is that coming from?" his question catches me off guard.

"Your actions…" He yells into the phone

"My actions… Ok, you're tripping now Vance… and I really don't have the energy to go back and forth with you while you nick pick because I'm late. I'm fucking running late, it's not the end of the world, but it is the end of the mood that I was in. So I guess we will try this at another time." I say as I make to uturn changing the course of my previous destination.

"Don't end the conversation now. I want the truth. Who are you fucking Dianah because you are not fucking me?" His words stung me. Sent me into a defensive mode and I came out swinging.

"The truth, the truth is… if I was fucking someone else Vance, you of all people should know that I wouldn't do it behind your back!" My words are sharp and direct, and add salt to an open wound that my leaving him in the past for other women created.

"Go to hell!" I hear the pain in his voice as he hangs up on me.

The moment I said it, I regretted it. I close my eyes and see the emotion. I remember each word we said to each other like it was yesterday. I want to call him back… tell him that I love him… tell him that he is the only man for me… ease him inside my womb so that he can feel the truth that he is the only one. But I don't. My temper is boiling and I won't cave under his insecurities. I have always supported him in his endeavors, and I expect him to do the same for me. I kick off my shoes and shake my head at his accusation. I can't help but feel a little guilt for the thoughts I have been having about Ramona knowing that they to play a part in my lack of intimacy with him. I'm a woman that believes in satisfying my lovers. So as for Vance's backed up aggression, I know that I have to step up my game. I start to peel away the blouse and skirt I was wearing, an outfit that Vance salivates over.

Bam… Bam… Bam.

I grab my black silk robe and conceal my black and red laced bra and panty set. I go to my front door and open it after glaring through the peep hole and walk to the center of the room. Vance locks the door, tosses his keys on the accent table a few feet away from the door. I look at my masculine lover's face and see his femininity clearly. I see where he has wiped his tears away and the moisture mixed with anger. He walks over to where I stand, looks at me, searches my silence for answers to the questions that are running through his head. His breathing is so heavy that his chest looks as though it is going to explode with each inhale. I know that my last words pushed him to his breaking point. Pushed him to come to my house unannounced, which I am not pleased with at all…in all the years we have been on and off, he has never just showed up. He grits his teeth as he touches my neck with his right hand, then lets his fingers trail the curve of my cleavage till they reach the center. I cut my eyes at him. Not in a sexual way, not at all. I cut my eyes to let him know that the things he said to me were still fresh in my mind and none of them weren't words of foreplay.

"You're kidding right?" My voice is more than conformation of my mood.

"Don't go there. We both said some things." He orders as he put his finger under my chin to tilt my head and make me meet his eyes.

"I'm sorry for being impatient with you, but I meant what I said, Dianah. And I'm not gonna apologize for that."

He begins kissing my neck. His touch seems so cold to me. It's not a touch of passion. This is the touch of a jealous man, not the touch that a man gives when he wants to erase all other remnants of past touches that do not belong to him but he knows exist.

"Aah…. Vance, wait." I pull away from him. I feel his anger build when I do but I continue to move away.

"What's up with that?" His voice is as deep as his emotion are right now.

"I'm sorry for what I said. I love you, I do, but I don't think we should go there tonight." I readjust my robe and fold my arms across my breasts. Vance's look makes me nervous for the first time in years. I'm a little apprehensive as he steps towards me.

"Baby, did you let someone touch you?" His eyes cut through me.

I watch at him watch me.

"I don't want to do this with you." I begin to walk away from where we were standing, trying to gain some space between us.

"Did you let someone fucking touch you… did you?" his yell is so loud that my insides vibrated. I turn to face him as he yanks me by my wrist.

"No… Vance I'm with you, and have been with you only." I reply even though I don't like this. I don't like the way this moment feels, the air is so thick.

"Then prove it!" Vance walks over to me and pulls open my robe. My breathing becomes short. I hold my hand up against his chiseled chest; feel his heart beat as he holds both sides of my face with his hands and kisses me roughly. I know that I haven't held up my end of the deal in the sex department lately, but I don't like this. Vance picks me up and carries me to our room, in my place, where all of our memories are framed and displayed like souvenirs that never leave the time capsule, and lays me on top of the bed. I want to tell him to stop as he pulls off his shirt and unfastens his belt, exposing his stubbornness, as his pants drop to the floor along with his boxers. I cover myself, trying to hide all of the emotions running wild inside of me right now.

"Uh-Uh…. I want to see you." Vance shakes his head as he yanks the covers from over me. Then he reaches for my panties. My reflexes work with my emotions and I place my hand on his to stop him.

"Baby please… not tonight. Can we just hold each other?" I hear my own voice crack.

"Humph…" Vance doesn't reply to my request. He just proceeds with more aggression. He flings the panties that were meant for his pleasure when I put them on, to the floor. He reaches for what we have always used and he stops in his tracks.

"Why is there a new box of Ecstasy's in here?"

"It was time to change them out, you know they had been in there awhile."

It's not the first time that I have replaced the box of condoms, but it is another first for him tonight in asking me why. If his look could kill, I would be a dead woman right now. I can see the muscles move in his chest and face as he covers his manhood. He rubs lube over the rubber and his skin. He opens my legs without tenderness and crawls in between them. He focuses on my face, watches to see if worry covers it. I don't know this side of him. I don't like it. I don't like what his actions implications. I don't want this right now. I'm his woman and he is my man, but I don't want this.

"Baby, please don't." I plead.

My words only enrage him and he presses his anger inside of me.

"Oh God… Ooh…" I lose my breath. I grab a hold of his shoulders, while my body shakes from pain underneath him. He watches me. His look is cold as he goes as deep in me needed for me to take all of him. I can't hide my displeasure with what he's doing to me, so I make it known.

"Vance, oooh… don't… ouch…" I use his broad shoulders to push myself up and ease him out some.

"Stop fighting me, dammit, and give me what's mine." He says as he holds me by my neck with one hand and by my waist with the other, and fills my insides over and again.

"You drive me insane… I would go mad if you ever let another man inside of you." He says pressing his lips to my ear, then he releases the grip he has on my throat and kisses me. His strokes are long and deep. Each one more intense than the one before it. I try and hold back my tears, but they fall against my will. Vance sees that I'm crying and the air in the room shifts. I close my eyes and feel him pulling himself out of me some. I feel his lips kissing my neck softly. I feel his tempo slow down. I feel his rhythm change to the one I know… change to the one I love to feel. I feel the warmth of his tears run down the meaty part of my breasts as he sucks on my nipple. I feel his anger change into desperation. I open my eyes and see his need to be all I need… all that I crave in this world.

"I love you… tell me you love me. Dianah please… tell me you love me!" He pleads with desperation.

"I… Oooh… shit…Ooohh… love… baby… Oooh… you… damn…Ooh… damn." I managed to get the words out as he deep grinds me, trying to move things that have always seemed to remain inside me. I shake from his emotion. I feel his vein pulsate against my walls.

"Omg… baby…" He moans Vance's eyes open and close. He moans and mumbles words that are unclear to me.

"Oh God…" he pleads to the heavens above. I dig my nails into the skin on his ass, and he cries out. Tells me how much he loves me, he tells me how much he needs me, he tells me how he wants me, He begs me to be his only. He vows to be mine always. Then he does another first in our relationship, he's Cumming slow and controlled inside me. He's not even pushing himself in completely. The throbbing of his tamed release is bringing me to a heightened state. I work my ass in a slow grind of my own. I make him shake on top of me. I feel his body flinch but he does not weaken all the way inside of me.

"Stay with me baby..." I order and he does as I command him to do.

"Yeah... that's right baby... stay with me." I know when I talk to him, it excites him. So I do until he is fully erect again. I cover him with my liquid heat. Making sure every inch of him is lubricated. "Let me get on top."

He jerks as he leaves my warmth and hits the chill in the air. I smile at his reaction, and then I mount my stallion carefully. I ride him slow and easy. He cries out, grips the sheets, arches his toes, bites his lips. All of the anger he entered me with is gone. My body working away all the tension that had built up. I look at my man, play with his nipples with my tongue, and scratch his skin.

"Oh...oooh... fuck..." Vance is lost in my rhythm and I make him enjoy the beat. I suck on his neck, lick his ears, make him hold out, make him ache inside me, make him apologize for his earlier actions; I make him beg me to cum, then make him beg me to stop. I make him weak, and then give him strength until he is numb. Until his eyelids no longer stay open on their own. Then I remove his weakness, get a warm wash cloth and clean him while he sleeps. Then I take a shower and cleanse myself.

Ivory Dinero

I blow out the smoke that transpires from the pull of my cigarette. It floats to the top of my head and lingers in the mix blend of cigarettes, cigars, and gunja from the other paying patrons inside of Bareback. I slip a crisp dollar bill inside the bikini string thong of Fantasy from the stack of five hundred that rest next to my half drunken drink, as she glides her plush spot down my thigh and her bare nipples across my lips, like my smoking doesn't bother her. She acts more like the smoke adds to the illusion the dim lights and alcohol provides, all trinkets that masks the acts of the individuals engulfed in the atmosphere. For the strippers, it conceals the blemishes in their skin and on their souls, making it easier to smile and entice the mystique demeanors of fathers behind on child support, passing bills through their teeth, husbands that are either afraid of bringing the freaky side of them out to their wives or those that can't get their wives to do kinky sexual acts with them… so they pay a little extra to fulfill their needs in the pink room before returning to their routine lives. To the women that are just as direct with intent on finding pleasure between the thighs of a stripper as the next nigga, I mean…. They're taking advantage of ladies' night like Remy and I are and have been for the past few months now and with Diamond's discounts … "Champagne room anyone?"

"Do you want to take this to the champagne room now?" Fantasy whispers in my ear with each word dripping with seduction.

"You know me too well." I say as I run my hand down her ass. As she carefully stands up in front of me with a smile on her face, then looks at Diamond and gives her a head motion towards the curtains that lead to the champagne room and Diamond's face lights up with excitement as she taps Remy on her knee.

"Let's get it poppin' Ivory." Remy says to me as we stand at the same time.

"I'm ah make it rain!" I reply looking at the perfection that goes by the stage name Fantasy. Fantasy is five foot seven, one hundred and sixty five pounds. Her medium brown skin shines under the dim lights. Her wet & wavy hair rides the line in her back ending at the top of her bootylicious ass that curves to her thighs. Her breasts are a full D cup and all hers, accented with nipples that stands out like stem less cherries.

The moment the door closed behind the manager's exit from collecting the payment for two hours and disbursing the funds to Fantasy and Diamond for their time, Diamond runs across the room and jumps into Remy's un expecting arms. They both crash land onto the black leather couch. Diamond wraps her arms around Remy's neck and plants a deep kiss on her. Fantasy smiles at her friend's corkiness then looks me in my eyes, runs her finger through the front of my spiked hair. Fantasy straddles me and in the softest tune says. "I'm glad that you could get away tonight!"

I crank my eye at her "Could... I come and go as I please." I say to her as though the time we share is not confided to this club and the different rooms in it.

"I didn't mean it like that... I... I was looking forward to seeing you last week that's all..." She bites on her bottom lip slightly and all the emotion that Fantasy tries not to show is clear.

I remove one of my hands from her bottom and touch her face. "I had to work late that night all hell had broken loose over a project that did not meet its deadline!"

"I understand." She says then she nibbles on my bottom lip, before sucking on my tongue. Fantasy lets out a moan and bites me on my neck, as she plays with the zipper on my Perry Ellis jeans. Fantasy sits up and looks down at what she now holds in her hand with a devilish grin just before she slides it inside of her. Fantasy tilts her head back as my extension fills her inside. Fantasy grips my shoulders and bares down on me to gain the position she needs to make her wetness wetter.

"Yeah make it rain," I say as I wrap my fingers around her throat and pull her down hard. Her body shakes and her words and moans join Diamond's.

"Harder, do it harder! Fantasy states her desire without reserve, even though we weren't alone. I love her honesty about what she likes.

"Who's pussy is this?" Remy ask Diamond in a cocky tone.

"It's yours… all yours daddy!" Diamond assures Remy in between the squeals that come out from underneath Remy's chest as the sweat on Diamonds back makes her stick to the squeaky lather and her leg bounces freely on the side of Remy's.

The bubbles in the Champagne room rise to the top for about an hour and a half before Remy and I readjust ourselves before we sit back and relax while Fantasy and Diamond go to freshen up.

"She rides my dick like she's making a baby!" I look at Remy for understanding and she gives it.

"Bruh… bitch be trying to kill a nigga. If we weren't here, she'd still be on my shit!" Remy says and we both shake our heads and let out a side grabbing laugh.

Diamond and Fantasy make their way back smelling and looking as fresh as they did when we first saw them tonight. I couldn't help but think about how easy it was for them to erase the signs of what we just did within minutes. I wonder if Fantasy has done this for some other woman tonight. I know that she is the fantasy that many want to fulfill. Fantasy swore to me that she was not having sex with any of her other clients. I sometimes find that hard to believe but she doesn't have a reason to lie to me. Seeing that she didn't want to have anything beyond a lap dance to do with me when I told her I was in a relationship. Then one night a few months ago Fantasy was having a really hard night dealing with a group of ignorant men that were having a bachelor party and the groom-to-be set his sights on Fantasy. The groom was all over her to the point where the bouncer had to give him a rough warning to sober him up some. So I approached her with the offer of going to the champagne room so she could take a break from the madness. After weighing her options, Fantasy agreed to take me up on my offer. I paid the manager and we drank champagne as we talked about things in our lives. Over the past few months Fantasy and I have grown closer than either of us expected. Fantasy told me about her brief encounters with dudes in her teenage years while she tried to figure out why she desired women. She told me about her past relationships that didn't last most of them do to her profession. She told me how working at Bareback has paid for three years of college already.

"What are you thinking about? Fantasy asks as she sits closer to me examining my expression.

I didn't want to let her into my thoughts so I shake them off. I gave her a light kiss and pour her another glass of champagne. Fantasy feels my evasive intent so she takes a sip of champagne and lays her head on my shoulder. I love the way she never presses issues with me.

"Bay, you got a nigga starvin' up in this piece!" Remy says as she rubs her stomach that we all hear rumbling.

"I don't have to ask if you want to grab a bite to eat!" I say in a joking manner as I get up and kiss Fantasy long and hard. Her eyes ask if she will see me Friday but she does not question me about my time. "That's for you." I say as I direct my eyes to the white business card with my number on it that I left on top of the four hundreds and ninety-nine one dollar bills on the table as her tip. She brandishes a wide smile as she picks up the card and presses it to her chest.

"Remy, I'll be in my car" my words tell Remy to make her hustling Diamond out of her hard earned money quick. "We'll talk later." I say as I make my exit knowing that Fantasy doesn't like to think of me going home to share my life and my bed with another woman, No more then I like to think of her doing this with someone other than me.

What's Done in the Dark

I examine her face and the veins that spring out of their hidden places on her neck. Examine the way she bits her lip, count the number of lines that forms between her closed eyes, each one deep, each one having their own story to tell. I examine her exposed breast and their fullness. I take in her moans as she lets them out into my space. I glance around my guest room focusing in on the framed memories of Vance and I that I kept in this room alone, the other side of me, then to the coats that were no longer on the bed but all over the floor. I allow my eyes to be a witness to the completely naked dark tone shape of the woman in between her legs as her locks cover parts of her inner thighs and the face of the culprit that was the cause of her erotic gestures. Remy moves her head and body in slow motions as she sucks and licks Ebonee with animated slurping sounds. Ebonee must have sensed my presence because she opens her eyes and looks directly at me. She doesn't tense up or make Remy aware of my presence, nor does she try to cover up her act of infidelity even though her lover and my friend sat a few feet away in my living room. Our eyes held each other captive for a moment then I close the door and walk away from what my ears overheard… what my eyes took in but were not meant for me to see… their hidden secrecy. My mind is running a million miles an hour. What the fuck did I just walk in on? This is definitely a catch twenty two. If I tell, I break the confidence of one of my friends. But if I don't, I betray the other. I walked to the living room mentally notating everyone's whereabouts. Chase, Kioni, Ivory, and Cameron are occupied at the card table. Raven is in the kitchen refilling her glass of wine. Raven!

"Pour me a glass!" I state as I hurry my way to her side.

She can see in my face that something is up.

"What's up?" she asks as she hands me the glass of red wine and took a sip of hers. I drink half the glass without removing the glass from my mouth or taking a breath. Then I grab Raven's hand and lead her to the backyard.

"I just walked in on Ebonee and Remy fucking in my guest room." I say trying to gain company in the uncomfortable position I find myself in. Raven takes the content of her glass to her head before she gave a response to the information she just received.

"Did you just say Ebonee?" Raven questions.

"Yes."

"And Remy?"

"Yes."

"Having sex?"

"Yes, butt booty naked!"

Raven takes my half full glass out of my hand and drinks it. She holds her chest with her empty glass pressed against the center of her chest as though the wine were sitting in that spot and not running rapid through her blood stream.

"Do they know that you saw them?" she asks after the delay with her feedback.

"Ebonee looked me right in my eyes and didn't miss a beat. She didn't even try to cover her breasts or anything."

"Girl, they were going at it like that?"

"Hell, Remy never even noticed that I was there. Her ass was so deep into Ebonee's nookie."

"Stop playing ...Di!"

"I wish I was playing... As hard as I'm wishing that she gains a hint of common sense and cleans herself up and returns to the party before Ivory begins to look for her."

"In what fantasy world would Ivory get up from a game of cards, let alone look for Ebonee?" Raven sucks her teeth.

"That's cold!" I say with empathy.

"Yeah it is, but it's the truth..."

"The shit Ebonee is doing is still foul as hell!"

"How dare they have no regard for Ivory or me and do this in my house!" I began to get livid as the level of disrespect starts to sink in.

"I know... they could have gotten a room somewhere... this is straight up trifling!" Raven states as she shakes her head.
"And this is clearly not the first time..." I snap.

"You think not?"

"Think... I know it's not... they were too familiar with each other and unguarded with their actions."

"I would have never in a million years suspected... Ebonee and Remy...Remy and Ivory go back years... you would think that there would be some form of loyalty among the two of them!"

"I can't believe you even use the word loyalty in the same sentence with the name Remy. I always knew that she was grimy but I didn't think she would stoop this low!"

"I need another drink." Raven holds up her hand and reenters my house. I peer into the dining area focusing in on Ivory at the card table smiling at the hand she holding, oblivious to the other game she was playing in. I wonder how a person could be in a relationship with someone and not feel them fucking someone else a few feet away from them. I slide the glass door open to let Raven back out with our completely full glasses of Sangria, which would be over kill under any other circumstance. I take a few swallows from the glass she hands me.

"So, when are you gonna tell Ivory?" Raven ask.

"How am I gonna tell her that her "boy" is fucking her woman? I mean I know that she is a neglectful lover and may have even pushed Ebonee into the arms of another but…"

"But nothing! Ebonee and Ivory are both adults and if Ebonee wanted to be with someone else, she should have been a grown up and ended things with Ivory first! As for Remy she has reached a new level of low in my book!" Raven sternly states taking another sallow of her drink.

"This is a very selfish and blatant act on their part and it's going to affect more than the three of them. I don't want to be the bearer of bad news. You know people always get angry with the one person that is honest with them instead of the ones that has been keeping up the lies!" I say with the realization of the impact that truth brings.

"So sad… but true!" I shake my head.

We both look at Remy walk over to the table with a smirk on her face, a drink in her hand, and make conversation with her friend without a hint of remorse for her actions.

"That's wrong on so many levels!" I say as we both shake our heads in disbelief.

Then Ebonee spots us on the porch and begins to make her way toward me.

Ebonee Price

I hid my lies behind Ivory's lies until I no longer felt remorse about them, now that mine are exposed, it seems as if the walls around me are caving in. I thought that I would feel better knowing that my actions would cause Ivory the same pain that she caused me. I even thought about telling her a few times… mostly when she was primping in the mirror just before she would leave the house or right after she would ease in the bed at four in the damn morning but it was never my intent for her or anyone else to find out like this. I don't know what I was thinking… I don't know how I went from being scared of telling my Ivory my wants to laying on top of my Dianah's guest bed staring her in her eyes without a blink, while my lovers best friend ate me out knowing full well that Ivory was in the dining room. I don't know maybe some part of me wanted it to be Ivory that came looking for me. Maybe some part of me wanted Ivory to see firsthand where her broken promise to love me brought me. Maybe some part of me wanted my betrayal to cut a wound as deep as the one my first and only love has given me. I'm on an emotional rollercoaster with Ivory's lies on one side of my mind and my pain on the other. I close my eyes and breathe in deep. I feel the temperature in my body rise as I feel the tightness of my chest try and contain the erratic rhythm of my hearts pounding beat. I step real slow while I try and think of what I can possibly say to my friend about my careless actions but no words come to mind, only the look in Dianah's eyes appear from moments ago when she saw me indulging in a lustful moment and I nearly burst into tears. I swallow hard as I get closer to the sliding glass door that leads to the porch where I see Dianah and Raven talking. I want to turn around and run free from the repercussions of my actions, but Kioni is right behind me. I have no room to turn and sprint away, so I open the door and silently count to three as Kioni closes it behind me.

"Are you going to tell Ivory you're fucking her or do I have to tell her what I just walked in on? Dianah folds her arms firmly in front of her and continues talking without giving me the time to reply. "If you are unhappy in your relationship to the point that you have to step out on Ivory, then Ebonee you should have at least done it with someone other than a person she considers a friend… and definitely not in my house right under her nose. That was not only disrespectful to Ivory but also disrespectful to me!" Dianah's eyes leave me and go to Kioni as I hear her gasp at Dianah's comment.

"She is fucking Remy!" Raven and Dianah spit out in unison. Their words catching Kioni by surprise and cut through my flesh like a jagged blade as the social acknowledgement of Remy and I clung to the air and regret set itself free through my pores. Out of all the reactions, Kioni' s is the one I fear most because I'm closer to her than anyone else in the circle of women that I have had the privilege to call friends. Kioni took me under her wings, so to say, when I met her a little over two years ago and I not only admire her but have formed a genuine sisterly love for her. So I nervously look for my pack of cigarettes that I know is somewhere in the bottom of my Coach bag. After fumbling through its contents, I find them and light one as quickly as I can.

"Oh… My … God… Ebonee why? Why would you sleep with Remy knowing that she and Ivory are close friends? Do you know how hurt she is going to be when she finds out that the two of you have been betraying her like this? Wait… Ebonee… please tell me that's not why you chose Remy to sleep with in the first place?" Kioni asks me in the big sister tone that I've come to know and look forward to over the years.

"How could you fuck Remy with Ivory literally feet away from you? You are acting like her fucking groupies…Willing to spread your legs wherever and whenever she is willing to take it because she has been in a few movie scenes!" Raven says with distain and disappointment in her voice just before I reply to her and Dianah's verbal attacks.

"I didn't mean to have sex in your house Dianah… and for that I apologize. I truly hope you can forgive me for doing that. As for Remy what, what can I say. We didn't plan on catching feelings for each other and I'm not even sure when or how we did. I'm not gonna try to justify my actions tonight because no matter what I say I can't. I can honestly say that I tried everything within my power to work things out with Ivory before it came to this, but I seem to be the only one willing or trying to make our relationship work. I know that you guys are trying to look out for your Ivory but she has played her part in this too. Maybe she is too settled in her ways… or maybe I'm too busy trying to create my own path… I lost track on who should be hurt or which one of us is to be blamed… all I'm clear on is that Ivory and my relationship is at the point where we can't say how we feel without arguing… and we can't argue without it turning into a fight!" I wipe away the evidence that I once cared for Ivory as my tears begin to fall. I light another cigarette.

"Ebonee, You promised… Her words remind me of the promise I made to her to try and cut down my smoking. you know that chain smoking isn't good for your health… Kioni looks at me the way a mother looks at her child when she knows that the consequences of their bad decision is going to hurt them more than any punishment she issues will.

"Neither is sleeping with your lover's best friend!" Raven sucks her teethe behind her words.

"Ray," Kioni's gesture pleads with Raven to ease up on me.

"I'm sorry Kiki … I know it's usually my job to approach things from a understanding and logical stand point … but I'm not getting paid to help her focus on her center pain…Ebonee, you are dead wrong on so many levels… Come on, you chose her friend out of all the women out there … You sleep with her in a mutual friend's house with your lover in the next room… And to top it all off … I can smell Remy's freaking cologne on you from here!" Raven flung her words through the air like bullets aimed right at me.

"I can smell it too…That's trifling… hell… for that matter how are we to know or believe that Remy is the only one you had your sights on? You did break the circle of trust when you fucked her!" Dianah turns her lips up at me then looks at Raven and Kioni.

"Good point!" Raven says as she through her hands up and let them drop heavily to her sides.

"You did break the barrier of trust, Ebonee." Kioni agrees with Dianah and I feel the sting on the left side of my chest like I have just been branded like the woman in the Scarlet Letter and my emotions fly like my fist usually do.

"How dare you! How dare you make me out to be a bitch in heat fucking any and everything moving! I have never looked at Cameron or Chase in that way and I never would!" I am so full with anger and hurt from the accusation to realize that I'm screaming… Or that footsteps are vastly making their way to the porch from the inside, I look at Kioni. "Kioni, you know how much I value your friendship right… I wouldn't do that!" I search for clarity in her eyes.

"I'm sorry Ebonee. I only know what you allow me to see but your actions today are the total opposite of what you've shown me. Oh no!" Kioni says and puts her hand on her forehead to prepare for the fireworks as Cameron, Chase, Ivory, and Remy made their way on to the porch.

Kioni's words make me wish I could disown the things I've done. Make me wish there was some way I could erase the mistrust that my sleeping with Remy caused. Make me wish I could restore the dignity that my acts have stripped away. I look at Remy and reality rushes in on how lust quickly transforms in to consequence. I look at Ivory, the woman that promised to love me and that I willingly sacrificed to love and the thought of me losing the only friend I have makes me hate her even more.

"Ebonee… what's wrong?" Ivory ask me as she squints her eyes at me like it would allow her to see the cause of my tears before my words tell her.

"Fine … fine I will be the heartless bitch that you all see me as!" I say in a calm voice although inside my emotions are all over the place.

"What the fuck is going on?" Ivory snaps at me and I feel heat flush through my body.

"I've been fucking Remy for months now!" My words are as cold as my heart has become and I watch Ivory's face turn from red to pale

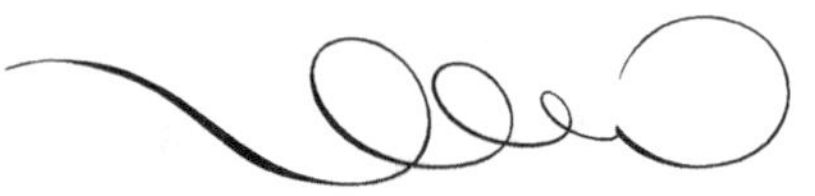

Ivory Dinero

"**I** have been fucking Remy for months now!" It's taking me a minute to process what Ebonee just said to me... Not because the words she used were in her native tongue or anything... But because the fact that Ebonee just told me that she has been fucking one of my best friends has me in a surreal state of mind. I feel the heat of my flesh rise off my checks and dance at the outskirt of my forehead. I see the faces of my friends and hear their voices around me.

"Please tell me that she didn't say that she has been sleeping you!" Chase questions Remy with the hope that Ebonee was referring to another person entirely.

"It just happened..." Remy's voice is nonchalant and filled with entitlement.

"Remy, you are a piece of work!" Dianah says as she heard Remy's lame excuse for betraying her friend.

"Hell, I thought that you of all people would understand that!" Remy says as she looks at Cameron for support.

"Hell nah ... man you know that shit isn't even cool! Things happen but there are things that never should happen and this is definitely one of those fucking things that shouldn't have every went down Remy!" Cameron says aggravated by Remy's tone and thoughtless actions.

"Excuse the hell out of me for being human! Remy spits out sharply.

"Get the fuck out of here with that shit..."Cameron says and waves her hand to shoo away Remy's violation.

"Being human has nothing to do with the dirty way you been doing your shit!" Kioni cuts her eyes at Remy.

"It's not like I wanted Ivory to find out like this…" Remy says as though finding out another way would have made all the difference in my understanding of her fucking my girl.

"And which way would you have preferred Ivory to find out Remy… By walking in on you eating Ebonee's pussy instead of me… or by smelling Ebonee's juices on your face?" Dianah snaps at Remy… But her words tell me that this isn't a moment of confession on Ebonee's part. That they were fucking tonight! I feel myself filling with rage.

"I am sorry, are you for the pussy or dick this week? Remy snaps at Dianah sarcastically.

"How did you except me to find out? What did you think that we would kick it, have a few beers and watch the game, then trade stories on how well she rides a dick during the commercials?" I step in between them looking my once close friend in her eyes… searching them to see if I see any part of a soul and fail to locate it.

"Don't take it there bruh… It's not even that type of party!" Remy says as she shots me a mean mug. And before I know it, I lunge at Remy with my fist flying. My right misses Remy's head by a few inches but my left catches her in the center of her cheek and she counters with a right left combo of her own that stuns me for a brief moment, then I charge her, taking her to the ground where I deliver more gut wrenching blows.

"Ivory, no! Please stop. I never wanted this." I hear Ebonee cry out.

"Baby stop them!" Kioni screams for Chase to restore some form of order in the mist of this chaos.

"No let them fight it out!" Chase adamantly replies.

"Nah, right is right. Let her get in that ass!" Cameron's voice shifts as if she is trying to keep Ebonee and Kioni at bay.

My balled up fists pour down on Remy the way that my tears began to. I become blind, just as blind as I was to what was going on right in front of me. Remy uses my emotions to her advantage, flipping me over, straddling my waist, and wipes my tears with her knuckles.She delievers a few haymaker blows before Cameron and Chase Have a change of heart and pull her off of me.

"Ivory you had me, but you were the one to let me go. So I don't understand how you have the nerve to actually fight her like you care…" Ebonee says as she grabs my hand and helps me up off the ground. In this moment I wish that I weighed far less than I do so that I could push her fucking hand away and spare myself the extra blow to my ego of being helped off the ground.

"I do care bitch… but you're too busy fucking my best friend to know that!" My words are full of all the hurt and embarrassment I feel.

"You care now that you have an audience but whenever I told you that you were hurting me, us… you never seemed to care!" Ebonee yells back at me, letting go of my arm forcing me to stand on my own two feet.

"Don't you see my fucking tears?" I throw my hands up with little force because I'm still winded.

"Well, since you're in such a caring mood tell me something Ivory…" Ebonee looks at me with water refilling her eyes as fast as it trails her face. "Was her pussy worth the love you promised me? Oh, you look surprised like I couldn't know. You would think that with all the caring you got going on you would want to come clean… that would be the mature thing to do, right?… but wait, then that wouldn't leave me standing alone in the center of this wrong now would it? Funny thing is, I use to think that I couldn't live without you Ivoy... without you loving me... I even started to believe you when you said that no one would even want me... but while she was holding me I got over you... I got over your touch then I got over the lack of it..." Ebonee steers at me allowing me to see all the pain that I have filled her with.

I feel my heart nuzzle into my throat as I think of Remy telling her all the details about Fantasy. I'm pissed that Remy slept with Ebonee... but to go against the grain and dime me out in order to do it is unforgivable. So I answer Ebonee with a question of my own. "Did Remy tell you about her before or after you fucked her?"

"Go to hell man!" Remy yells and points her finger at me from over Cameron's shoulder as Cameron holds her back. Her eyes water like the thought of me thinking that she would dime me out hurt her more than me finding out she slept with my woman did.

"Come on, you don't want to do this... ya'll have been boys for far too long!" Cameron says as she practically carries Remy a few feet away from me.

"Wait, Remy, you knew that she was cheating?" Ebonee questions Remy as she moves towards her lover with anger and betrayal etched across her face. "Well, I guess you were right Kioni, we only see what people allow us to see." Ebonee says as she walks past me, back into Dianah's house, and out the front door. I want to chase behind them both when Remy follows suit... But my pride keeps me still.

"Damn Ivory, we were out here defending your honor on the trifling shit she was doing to you and you are kicking up dirt in your own sand box... I can't believe that this is what love in our community has been reduced to... I seriously need a drink!" Raven shakes her head at me and walks towards the glass doors.

"Fuck the drink, it's time for shots!" Dianah says as she blows out air from her mouth, making a hissing sound in my direction and catches up with Raven as she makes her way through the door.

"I'm gonna have a few of those shots. When you come inside I'll patch you up… because I love you…although I don't really like you right now!" Kioni touches my hand briefly, shakes her head and joins Dianah and Raven inside.

"The two of them getting together was wrong… but two wrongs don't make a right… You can only push a person away so long before they leave on their own." Chase scolds me as soon as the door closes behind her woman entering the house.

"I told you that Karma never plays favorites in the game of life!" Cameron's words knock the wind out of me.
In my heart I know that they are all right.

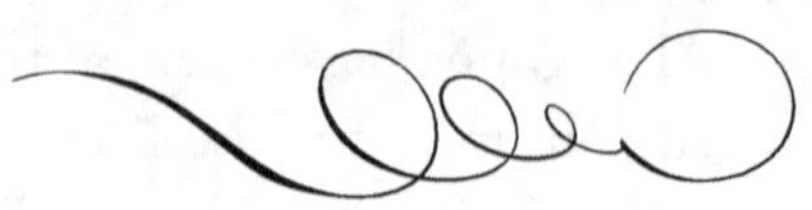

Kioni Wils

"Slow down before you choke yourself" Chase says to Deshaun and shakes her head at the way he is swallowing down a fork full of scrambled eggs with cheese, a whole piece of bacon, and a bite of strawberry jam toast at the same time.

"Ma, Dee will be here to pick me up for practice any minute now!" Deshaun says as he picks up his orange juice and gulps down what was left in the glass. Then he picks up his empty plate and places the dishes in the sink beside me.

"Thanks for breakfast mommy!" he says with a smile and plants a kiss on my cheek.

"You're welcome, Booboo!" I return the smile with a slight laugh because he's spoiled, and he knows it. My thought is broken by the honking in the driveway of his best friend's father since grade school Derrick. And I know its Rich driving because had Keya been driving, she would have made her son get out of the car and knock on the door like the sensible young man he is.

"There's a couple of dollars for you on the counter, be careful!" I nudge my head in the direction of the bills and advise in my usual motherly tone.

"Yes mam!" Deshaun replies as he picks up the money and stuffs it into his gym bag.

"Love you mom!" Deshaun says to chase.

"I love you more!" Chase replies as she watches Deshaun exit. Then she folds and places the sun sentinel on the table. Chase reaches up and receives the freshly poured cup of caffeine-free coffee with cream and two and a half tea spoons of sugar I held out in front of her as I place her plate down in front of her.

"Mmm, this is so good!" she says with a smile as her eyes follow me as I sit down beside her with my own cup and breakfast in hand. I sip from my cup of coffee that's made exactly the same and agree with her. Chase takes a few forks full of her food, a bite of toast, and another sip of her coffee before she says "You know there are some things that we have to talk about."

"I know, after breakfast." I softly reply then I play with my eggs with my fork a bit before I look at her.

"You need to slow down before you choke!" I warn then we both fall out laughing because we know that's where Deshaun picked up his eating habits.

After I place the dishes into the dishwasher and turn the cycle on, I walk into the living room. Chase is sitting on the sectional in her gray wife beater and gray basketball shorts with the white and1 emblem on the bottom right corner. I walk over to her and ease in front of her placing the back of my soft white cotton t-shirt against her breast. Chase rests her back on the sectional arm then wraps her arms around me. Her warmth comforts me so I lean my head back on her left shoulder close my eyes and exhale.

"You know that you are not alone anymore, right?" chase questions me as she places a soft kiss on my neck.

"I know..." I reply as I open my eyes and look to the ceiling.

"It's your decision on how you want to deal with things...but keep in mind that you are not that little girl in a desperate time anymore." I feel her arms hold me tighter.

"I'm so tired of running" I feel the tears stream my face as I think of what I have to face.

"Then stop...from this point on we stand and fight until it's over!" Chase says as she looks at me then kisses me on the corner of my left eye as my tears lubricate her lips.

"I use to have dreams that he found us..." I pulse and whip away the tears that quickly get replaced. "And in the dream he takes him away from me..." I fill my emotions rash through my body and cause me to shake.

"If you let me help you with this, No longer will the steels be able to seal your peace or reappear to hunt your dreams... I promise you that!" Chase eyes locks on mines the intensity behind them makes me feel safe.

"Ok I trust you with this baby, but I don't want Deshaun to know... I don't think I could take it if he knew... or if he hated me. " I'm so full of conflicting emotions but his not knowing I'm sure of.

"Babe, he would never hate you, you are his mother... he loves you."

"That's because he doesn't know the things that I have done... that I had to do... he can never know... Baby, never!" I exclaim as I turn my body and look at her. I search her face to make sure she knows telling Deshaun is out of the question.

"We can handle the steels without Deshaun knowing anything but..."

"But what" I cut her statement short.

"But... in order to end this once and for all the paternity will have to be established..." Chase's tone is soft but clearly non-negotiable.

"Baby..." I cry out to my lover. My one word is full of fear and panic. They mix and send a rush of heat that causes me to stand. Chase gets up as quickly as I do. She takes my hand and looks at me. Her eyes are gentle yet full with purpose.

"Trust me. I will take care of you and our son, and I do mean our son. No matter the DNA strain, he will always be my son!" Chase says as her eyes let go of the liquid pain she was holding back until now.

"He is your son, in all the ways a child can belong to a parent. Deshaun is more like you then he is of me." I say as I cup her face with my hands and brush away the wetness falling from her eyes.

"I wish..." Chase gets out before I hug her tightly. I know that she wishes that our love alone could have been the cause of Deshaun's existence. I told her many times that our love did create the well-rounded child that he is today. I kiss her softly then hold her tight. Because I wish that too... more than anything I wish that too.

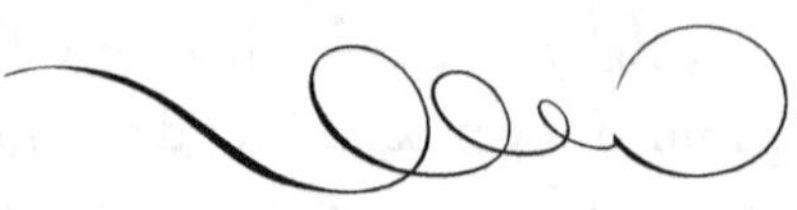

Raven Winters–Carver

I inhale the scent of the beautiful arrangement of flowers as I run the tip of the engraved card across my bottom lip. I think of Ndia the woman that has gone from sharing my bed occasionally to sharing my life with for months now. I am so anxious about our weekend getaway that will start as soon as this work day is over. I look at the clock on the wall and I'm as envious of each second that comes to pass as I am of the memory of our last sexual encounter. I have a mental vision of Ndia finger fucking my beautiful Dom without reserve.

"Dr. Carver, your four o'clock is here." My receptionist's voice fills the room. I close my eyes, inhale, and then exhale slowly quieting the sounds of that moment in my mind.

I adjust my skirt and press the button. "Send her in please."

The door to my office opens and in walks Mrs. Tomas. A woman in her mid-forties with thighs of a goddess and a face of an angel walks in. She's not wearing her usual blue skirt suite with blazer. Today she has on gray jogging pants and a blue t- shirt. Her hair is in a ponytail exposing her age in its slowed state.

"Mrs. Tomas, the last time you were here you said that you felt ready to be intimate with your husband again after his infidelity." I pick up form where our last section ended.

"Yes" she confirms softly.

"How did that go for you?" I make note as I walk over to the easy chair that was positioned in front of the couch that she sat upright on.

"I did." She rubs her hands along the sides of her jogging pants and swallows hard.

"And how was the experience for you?" I ask as I push the top of my pen down to expose the tip and ready myself to write down key words that express emotions in her that she may or may not know about or need my help in facing.

"I could feel her in his touch. It was like she was right in between us. Even the way he moved inside me was different. I don't even know if the intensity that fueled his kiss when he kissed me, was for me… or if it was because he was in thought of what it was like when he was kissing her…" She looks away from me in hopes that I don't see the pain behind her eyes.

"How does that make you feel?" I ask as I read her body language.

"How am I supposed to feel? My husband is sleeping with another woman." She replies in a sharp tone as she looks me in my eyes.

"Whatever you feel is what you are supposed to feel."

"I feel like I don't know him any more… like what I have given him throughout the marriage has been mediocre at best! I feel, I feel less than what I should when it comes to pleasing him sexually." Mrs. Tomas looks like a woman that has had sex for the first time and it wasn't the dream she envisioned now she is left dumbfound and disappointed.

"What have you given him?"

"Me!"

"And you feel second-rate?" I dig.

"At best…" She shifts.

"Why do you feel inferior in quality?"

"Because when we first got together, we could never get enough of each other… and when we made love, he would tell me that he wanted to exhaust me until it was hard for me to keep my eyes open… and he would complete that task." She lets off a hit of a smile as she reminisces.

"And now?"

"Now all the things that I used to long to feel from him… When he does them, my body stiffens and my mind tells my heart that love has lost!" She wipes away the falling tears from underneath her eyes and unexpectedly draws her knees to her chest and plants her head against them and cries for a few minutes. I watch her let go of the pain that she has been holding on to throughout our prior sessions and long before. When she brings her head from its pressed position between her knees, she lays it sideways on them and looks at me. Her eyes are stripped of their age and searching mine for guidance.

"Is that how you feel Lorraine that love has lost?" I use her first name to make her identify with her own emotion, even though they are filled with pain, they are also filled with the truth that she needs.

"Yes!" She grips her legs tighter and rocks to coat the pain she is feeling from her answer.

"Why do you feel that love has lost?" I dig deeper.

"I used to think that our love would last forever, that I would never lose my desire for him… and that love would never allow me to act on any invitations of attractions that may have arrived throughout the years of us being together… that love would keep his desires home with me… but it didn't, it wasn't strong enough!" She wipes away her tears then her legs go down, her back straightens, her shoulders broaden.

"It wasn't strong enough?" I turn her statement into a question for her clarity and my own.

"He, He wasn't strong enough!" She looks at me with eyes that have changed from sad to bitter, seconds before the timer chimes loud signaling the end of her session.

"I guess I'll see you the same time next week?" She states fugitively.

"See Marie on your way out, she will confirm your date and time. And Lorrain, try and do something that you really enjoy this weekend." I say in a pleasant tone.

"I'll try, Doc." She says brandishes a half smile before exiting my office.

"Umm" The powerful streams of hot water spews from the wide heads of the double headed shower skillfully positioned on opposite ends of the shower walls. The pressure sooths the buildup tension from my work week and the three-and-a-half-hour drive in rush hour traffic I endured getting to our private suite in the keys within minutes.

"You are so tense" N'dia says to me then she squeezes more body wash into her hands and messages my neck. I let out a few moans before I place my hands against the smoked tile for balance.

" Sounding like that is going to get me started!" Cameron says while she slows the speed of her hand that was already slowly washing between N'dia's' legs causing N'dia to let out a long moan of her own.

"Oh, no Baby. Don't you dare, I'm starving!" I cut my eye back at both of them knowing by the way N'dia just parted my legs that things are about to heat up and if they do it will be hours before we stop.

"Okay, okay!" Cameron grunts and kisses N'dia on her right butt cheek.

"You still want Seafood?" N'dia asks as she removes her hand from between my legs.

"God, yes!" I reply desperately as N'dia kisses me on my shoulder. Then we all bust out in laughter because we all know that I am easier to deal with once you feed me.

I have plans of my own on how I want the first night of our weekend together to end so after dinner I excuse myself. I pull my twists up into a ponytail, I remove my robe, and I put on my strap. I light scents and white candles around the bedroom. I spread the container of pink rose petals over the king size bed. I rearrange the black leather sofa chair to where it's only a few feet away from the foot of the bed then I walk into the living room area of the suite in my white wife beater and my black girl boxers that clearly expose my bulge. I look at Cameron and give her a devilish grin. Cameron smiles at me then takes a drink of her red wine. I keep walking over to N'dia. I watch N'dias' expression closely and try to read the thoughts in her head because I have never used my strap on her. I stand in front of her. I trail her lips with my finer tip then I take them into my mouth one by one sucking on them soft and slow before I allow my tongue to connect with hers inside her mouth. I kiss her deep, pull her body close to mine, and she closes her eyes. I run my hand over her butt and feel the rhythm of her breathing change. I break the kiss, take her hand and lead her and Cameron to the bedroom.

"So this is what you were up to." N'dia squeezes my hand tight and looks at me.

"Very nice…" Cameron says then kisses my hand before letting it go and taking a seat in the sofa chair.

I look N'dia in her eyes and run the fingertips of my right hand down the left side of her face to her chin then tilt her head back and take her skin into my mouth. I suck slow and firm while I remove her sexy lingerie. I guide her to the bed and lay her on top of the rose petals before I cover her naked body with mine. We heat the room up with each kiss. I open her legs wider and grind my print between her thighs. I take my time tongue kissing the meat of her right breast before I suck on the nipple then I do the same to the left breast.

"Baby you feel so good!" N'dia says in a tone that tells me she is turned on.

I smile and make a trail of kisses down her stomach and inner thighs as I go down on her and work my magic with my tongue.

"Umm, Ooh, my" N'dia moans, grabs my head, and grinds her arousal on my tongue. I tongue fuck her deep, make her body perform tricks until she is drenching wet for me. I crawl up her twitching body and kiss her.

"I lost count on how many times you made me… What are you doing to me?" she questions in-between kisses

"Making sure you are ready" I say as I pull my strap out of my boxers, circle the head of it in her wetness a few times before I slide its thickness deep inside her warmth.

"Ooh, God, Raven" N'dia cries out my name lick she is confirming who I am and getting to know me at the same time. Her breathing becomes stagnant then she pulls me close and kisses me deeper than the times before.

The way her moans sound in my ear brings out the tomboy in me and I give her my tomboy in each stroke until she can't take anymore. I leave her with her legs numb and fighting to control the shaking of her body.

I put my tomboy back in my boxers and kneel down in front of Cameron. I pull down her basketball shorts and take her clit into my mouth. I suck her slow, make her grip the arms of the chair, make her lean her head back and curse and moan how good my tongue feels. I feel her body tense and shake, the signs that's she's getting close to her point and I stop just before her climax. Cameron opens her eyes to see the reason why.

"Come on," I reach out my hand and She looks at me with a hint of reluctance in her eyes but she takes it my hand and lets me lead her.

I walk Cameron to the bed and playfully push her down beside N'dia. I kiss N'dia who has been watching me with Cameron the same way that Cameron had been watching us and let her see how good their juices taste mixed together. I look at Cameron and I want to take her places she has never let me take her in front of any one before. And I don't want to ask her because I don't want to give her the option of saying no. So, I pull Cameron's shorts off of her completely and take her into my mouth again. I lick and suck her hungrily until she cums hard in my mouth. I lock her shaking legs in my arms tightly then sex her slowly with my tongue. Cameron's body twitches and her moans drive me insane. I let go of her left leg and enter her with two fingers.

"Ooh baby." Cameron cries out, her body tenses, and instantly she tries to stop my hand from going deeper.

"Relax" I say then I place the warmth of my mouth on her swollen part and suck it with the same tempo as I move my hand inside of her well, kept secret. Cameron lets out a moan mixed with both pleasure and pain, grips down on a pillow, and then loses her breath as I go deeper.

"You have me so turned on" N'dia whispers in my ear then kisses me on my shoulder.

"Is that so?" I look at my lover and I know what she's doing.

"Yes, you have me so ready for round two." N'dia leans her back against the leather head board and opens her legs like a beautiful butterfly, offering her body to me with the hope that I will spare her lover's.

Chase James

I walk through the toxic smell of decaying flesh and blood as I make my way down the hallway, passing uniformed officers that are doing their best to secure the crime scene so that the forensic team can do their jobs without tainting trace evidence. I cover my mouth and nose with a handkerchief as I walk into the master bedroom of the four bedroom home in Windsor Isles and the smell intensifies. I walk over to investigate the pale body that lay lifeless across the foot of a queen size bed. The hole in the upper right side of her brain supplied the blood puddle on the plush carpet below it. The way the victim fingers are gripping the comforter tells me that the victim, a Caucasian female who appears to be in her late thirties to mid-forties knew what was about to happen to her. I walk less than three steps before I'm standing over the head of a Caucasian male in his med to late forties and who appears to be the shooter based on the gunshot womb to his right temple and the twenty two caliber in his right hand. All the evidence points to homicide followed by suicide.

"James, you have to see this." My attention is pulled out of the room with urgency. By the look on my partner's face, I know it has to be bad.

"Sims, what is it?" I question my partner before we reach the destination because out of the year and a half of working with him, I've never seen him look so shook.

"This is not going to be pretty." Sims warns as he steps to the side of the door way. I instinctively bite down on my teeth to keep my emotions inside myself when my eyes take in the sight for themselves. The first thing to grab my attention is the lavender walls with a bright glossy trim. The trim matches the white side chair, bookcase, and toy chest that are placed through the room. Then my eyes set on the lavender tiny toons blanket with 'Babs' on it, and my heart skips a beat because I don't want to imagine let alone take in the sight that my job requires me to. I force my eyes to scroll up the tiny blanket and see the hands, lace pajama top, and face of a three to five year old angelic child that looks as if she is only sleeping but the small hole in the center of her head and red pillow case that use to be lavender tells the horrible truth. No sooner than my mind takes in the scene at hand Sims and I are called into another room. The walls are hospital white or maybe they appear to be because of the one off set black wall that had two different posters of the same band hanging on it. The white open stackable selves that lean against the black wall stores a radio, cds, music books, a game counsel, a basketball, and some free weights. On the white wall there was a black four sliding door cabinet with three open draw spaces at the bottom mounted on it. There are a few stickers sporadically placed on it. The cabinet had a couple of hats on the top of it and a gray guitar case that I can safely assume belongs to the black and white guitar on the stand below it. Then my eyes move along to the large black face clock with white numbers on it that hung just over the head of the full size bed that the lifeless teen between the age of thirteen and sixteen lays in. He too has a small hole in the center of his forehead.

"I need a minute," I say as I walk out of the room and make my way to the backyard of this half a million dollar home. I face the exotic trees that had to be shipped here and planted around the upscale heated pool. I think about how there are so many beautiful trinkets in and out of this house that mask the horror left inside.

"I was able to get in touch with the victims' family. It turns out that the husband and shooter, Jacob Sol, lost his job of fourteen years when the company he worked for went out of business six months ago. Family members say that Jacob became extremely depressed and isolated within the last month when he couldn't find a job and his savings started to deplete. They grew more concerned when the Sols didn't show up for Lily Sol's fifth birthday party a week ago." Sims says giving me the facts that lead up to this triadic event.

"From the looks of it she didn't make it to five. Let's get them out of here before the media sinks their fangs into this case." I shake my head at the thought.

"I can already hear the news now… President Obama has failed to create jobs in America!" Sims mimics a newscaster with his fist balled right below his mouth.

"Right… while they will fail to mention that there was a net loss of ninety-six thousand companies in the state of Florida alone in two thousand and nine and four hundred thousand in two thousand and ten according to the Bureau of Labor Statistics, which means America and its companies were in trouble way before two thousand and eight!" I say feeling like this man taking his whole family out and then himself because he lost his job… is as senseless as a world trying to blame one President for all the down falls in this country… the way I see it there are many to blame for the down falls they are just too high up to see… just like there are many positions available but people that are used to a high stature feel they could never going to lower themselves to menial work.

I walk in and touch the skin on Deshaun's face, still shaken by the images of the young victims in my case earlier today. I kiss Deshaun's forehead were the father placed a bullet in his children's, a little over two weeks ago. I watch my son sleep for a few minutes. I know that Deshaun is my son no amount of DNA or lack of it will ever change that… I exit Deshaun's room as softly as I entered it and walk into my newly decorated bedroom and place my 45 in its case and lock it away. I walk over to my lover, the woman that I love deeper than I have ever managed to hurt. I kiss her cheek softly and trace it with my fingertip for the first time since the last time I touched her without her permission. I realize that the connection made can be as damning or as powerful as love, because it is loves messenger. I make my way to the bathroom and close the door silently so I don't wake Kioni. I turn on the water to let it heat up while I undress. I step into the heated steam of the shower. I place my head under the hot water sprinkles of the shower head. I tilt my head back, letting the pressure of the streams revive the dried tear stains on my face and carry them away with the new ones. Kioni kisses me softly on my back and runs her fingers along my outsider shoulders. I didn't hear her enter the bathroom let alone the shower with me. Instinctively I turn around and her eyes greet mine as we stand face to face. I hold her venerability as tight as she is holding on to mine. I feel the stutter of her breathing on the inline of my neck and I know that she is crying too. We haven't been intimate since she told me about her molestation and I had to face the awful things that I have done to her as well. I loosen my grasp just a bit and let the sting of the water burn my eyes as I look at her. I take in the definition of love that she is extending to me in this moment. Kioni explains it through the gentleness of her touch as if she has never felt the harshness of mine. She carries it in her eyes each time she looks at me. I close my eyes and feel its power cover my soul. Then I lean down and kiss her with the deepest current of love in me. I feel Kioni pull me closer to her so I hold her as if my arms can melt away all of the pain of her yesterdays. We wash each other from the crowns of our heads to the soles of our feet letting all the shame and regret peel from our flesh and fall to the base of the tub with all the dead cells as they pore down the drain.

Kioni pours clarity into the palm of my hands and does the same to herself then we cover each other's body with the oil. Her skin shines with each flicker of the candle light of the candles on the dresser and nightstands she lit before she came into the bathroom. She lets out a few light moans as I trail her body with my fingertips. I step closer to Kioni and her breathing picks up along with my heart beat. I am as nerves to touch her as I was the first time we made love. Kioni looks at me, touches my face, rubs her finger slowly across my lips, and kisses me. The familiar of her tongue brings water to my eyes. Kioni runs her hands through my hair then back down to my face. She smiles with her mouth open and kisses me again. Kioni runs her hands down my neck, over my collarbone, and cups my breast, one in each hand and squeezes them firmly. Her breathing thickens as she rubs my nipples in between her fingers and so does mine. I kiss Kioni through my moans. I kiss her till my body sways with motion and hers build with desire. I drop to our bed with Kioni standing between my legs. I look up at my lover as she bends down to kiss me again. Her soft hair covers my face and shoulder. I draw her close to me, close my eyes, kiss her stomach, rub my face slowly across its smooth surface and let out a few moans of my own. Kioni takes my face into her hands and kisses me intensely. I finger the curve of her breast gently.

"I want you here!" Kioni says as she takes my hand and guides me to the center of her warmth.

"Are you sure you want me to? I question almost afraid of hurting her as she helps my finger inside of her heated wetness and lets out a light gasp. Kioni doesn't reply with words. She just kisses me hard and mounts me. She grinds her body against my hand. I Kiss then nibble on the skin of her cleavage. Kioni grabs my head and holds it pressed against her left breast while her body shakes on top of me and her heart pounds through her chest. When her body calms down and her arms relax around my head, I pick her up and lay her body on the bed. I hungrily taste the skin of her shoulder, neck, earlobe, and lips then I slide my hand back inside her warmth. I move with both haste and patience.

"I love you so much" Kioni says softly in my ear then heavy breathing and moans follow.

"I… love.. You" I tell her then I smother her sound with a half a dozen kisses or more. I feel the muscles in her body loosen. I feel her inner walls open then I feel her walls tighten around my fingers. I feel her pulse strengthen against my fingers before she inhales deep, shakes, calms, shakes, and then calms again.

"Oh my God…" I mumble then press my forehead against the back side of my hand that I hold on to the cream satin pillow case with as Kioni runs her nails slowly down the back of my neck, upper then lower part of my back, then over the curve of my behind. I shiver as I feel the heat of Kioni's tongue trail my spine.

"You feel so good" Kioni says as she nuzzles her head in her favorite body part on me, the curve of my back.

"Oh my… fucking… God…" I inhale as I feel Kioni peel apart the lips between my thighs and enter what is hers.

Kioni moans as though her soul is in agony. She kneads my flesh, kisses then bites me on my ass. She tells me to turn over and I do.

"I missed you." Kioni says as she looks me in my eyes and once again I am caught up in the rapture of her love. I brush the hanging hair out of her face and admire her beauty before she licks my lips, sucks on my neck, grips my breast and licks them while she holds them, Licks my stomach, runs her teeth below my belly line, then traces my clit with her tongue and takes my thickness into her mouth. Her desire for me takes my breath away. She likes the way I respond to her touch so she stops what she is doing to me, looks at me, and smiles.

"You like that?" She ask me in a confident tone.

"Key…" I call out as I feel Kioni place two fingers inside of me one after another forcing me to make room.

"I so want to fuck you…"Kioni says as she drives them deep inside of me causing me to squirm, causing my back to arch, and my legs to try and close.

"Ah.. Baby…" I try to ease away slightly but Kioni has a hold on me that will not allow me to. Kioni knows me, knows my body she covers me with the warmth of her mouth and tighten the lock she has my right thigh locked in then she pulls me on to her over and again. I close my eyes, hear myself moan, bite my lip, and turn my head from side to side. Kioni lets go of her hold and eases on top of me. She rubs her face into my neckline then places her hand firmly around it.

"Do you know how much I love you… How much I love making love to you?" She asks me as she sucks on a part of my neck that her hand didn't cover as she reenters me.

"Ooh… key.. baby…"I cry out in between breathes because it feels like she's fisting me.

"You know I would go insane if you ever let anyone else touch you like this…"Kioni states as she picks up her rhythm and personally delivers a wave of pleasurable pain to me.

"Ouch, baby…Yes,yes, I know" I say as I dig into her shoulders, grab the sheets and bunch them together, as Kioni causes my body to shake uncontrollably.

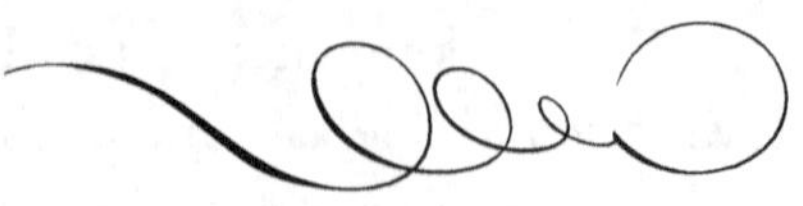

Dianah Marshall

I listen to the tone in Ramona's voice grow in assertion as she speaks to the pilot of her private jet that is also placed on delay just like all the other flights out of or into The Big Apple due to the weather. We had been negotiating terms with the investors of my new NYC project that launches the expansion of my business here all day when the weather took a turn for the worst. The heavy snowing that I find beautiful is now mixing with a down pour of icy rain and wind creating a hellacious storm. I don't have any complaints about the comfort level of the luxurious Loews hotel we are held up in till the weather clears up. I'm more concerned with the fact that Ramona's and my Suite are in such close proximity of each other. We have been in contact with each other daily either by phone or through e-mails for months now but not face to face. So I almost lost my mind when she walked into the meeting room in a black women's pants suit, silk black shirt with the two top buttons undone enough to show the indent of her collarbones and her hair pulled up and wrapped into a bun. Her presence was breath taken to say the least. I could feel my temperature rise all over my body and gather between my thighs every time she reached over me to retrieve or place a document on the long fogged conference table next to or in front of me and purposely let her arm touch me. I wanted to crawl underneath her clothes and trail her skin the way her light scented perfume eased through my nose and fondled my sense of smell. I have done all I could to keep my emotions in place when it comes to her, but I'm not sure how long I will be able to keep myself away from her. Ramona is the only woman that has ever made me long her in every way and I do mean in every way… to the point that I haven't let Vance near me because I feel like I'm being unfaithful to her somehow… and we haven't even kissed. Ramona and I have gotten closer to each other through conversations alone and she has made it very clear that she wants more than a business relationship with me.

"I enjoyed having dinner with you. thanks for staying awhile long." Ramona says after she ends her call and is close enough to me to brush against me and feel my body tense up. So she whispers in my ear "I can make you feel things that he never has if only you would let me!" I feel the heat of her words tap dance down my spine. I walk away from her and over to the mini refrigerator that is in the same location as the one in my suite behind the mini bar. I take out a bottle of water open it with my back towards her and take a few swallows trying to bring down the effects of the wine I had with my dinner we finished just before Ramona received her call.

"Dianah, Turn around and face me!" She orders a few feet away from me.

I turn and face her. Her essence is intoxicating and ignites the sexual tension inside of me and it explodes in the air like the thunderous roar of the wind that is smacking the windows.

"What are we doing?" I question knowing that I shouldn't be standing here in her suite… longing her touch… I gotta get out of here! But no sooner than my brain draws that conclusion Ramona is up on me. She removes the water bottle from my hand and places me against the wall. She lets her eyes embrace my light skin while she holds my arms over my head by my wrist. She leans in and kisses me deep for the first time. I can feel her heart beating as strong as mine. She sucks on my neck like she wants to consume the blood from the vein her tongue has a grip on. The thresh whole of her pleasure is everything I imagined and more but although I want to enter her realm I tell myself I have to stop.

"Wait. We can't. I can't!" I move away from her and create space between us by walking over to the window and the sound of the rain intensifies. I stare at the closed white blinds and readjust my white blouse and gray suit pants as I begin to talk to myself out loud.

"What the fuck are you doing Dianah, you're with Vance?" with or without sex… You are still in a relationship with him.

"But are you in love with him?" Ramona joins in the conversation I'm actually having with myself.

"I love him… He is in love with me…" I answer her with complete honesty.

"Are you in love with him?" Ramona repeats her question calmly as she closes the distance I set between us.

"He accepts me for who I am." I say sparking the memory of the day I told him I had feelings for women in my mind.

"He accepts you… and his acceptance is your binding obligation!" Ramona's words are filled with heavy emotion.

"You say you are ready to give me all of you… and I think about it… I do… but he wants to give me the same thing too… I'm so torn between you two!" I confess what I have been avoiding her finding out for months and turn away from my true desire.

"Ok then tell me this one thing. Do you look at him full of desire, the way you look at me?" Ramona asks as she moves in closer to me and lets her breast press against my back before interlocking her chocolate fingers within the tan fingers on my left hand that lay nervously on my outer thigh.

"Please don't touch me there!" I plead as she kisses me softly on the back of my neck in the spot that makes my body cry out for more.

"Where… right here?" she asks sensually as she slowly traces the spot with her tongue and sucks the skin in that area into her warm mouth.

"I know what you want from me and I'm just not sure if I can give you what you are asking for… Ramona if we… Everything… will change… Oh GOD…" Everything logical in my mind is telling me I have to pull it together… But I don't want her to let me go!

"Why don't you, let my liquid desire, prove to you, how much I long you?" Ramona questions in an aroused state planting kiss after kiss on my neck after each word.

"Forgive me for what I'm about to do." I whisper to the heavens before I turn around and take Ramona in my arms the way I have done countless times in my dreams.

Ramona's back arches. Her ebony hands tighten into fist gripping the sheets, pulling them from their corners with each pleasure-induced lick I give. I run my tongue slowly along her natural design, from its beginning to the middle were I linger teasingly, tasting her outer and inner sweet with prolonged licks and sucks, causing her ebony frame to shake and intoxicating sex moans to rise from silence. Her moans filling my ears and the room dimly lit by the night lights that brightly light up the streets and park Ave, yet barely easing their neon glow through the blinds as did her sexual arousal in my mouth, caressing the waves of ecstasy our bodies movements causes, as we break through the mass of indifference and time giving into desire. She feeds me for the third time. Her hips the round spoon, her navel indented, nipples erect, breast as smooth as silk, her mouth as tight as her bottom lip pressed against her teeth, nose flared as she inhales life and its freedom with each breath, eyes closed, all its beautiful decoration. I indulge hungrily as she takes the back of my head into her hands and grinds into my face making sure that I get my full serving. Heat covers my exposed naked as she straddles me wildly. I watch as she works her brown sugar deep, circling then back up to the tip of my fingers without removing her warm erotica completely. It's throb pulsing with that of the beat of my heart. Both in their own race… Her prize being another climax… She being mine. She collapses on top of me. She smiles as her head rests on my shoulder. She removes the few strains of jet-black shoulder length hair that fall over her eye disturbing her view of me. Her breathing stables somewhat and she tells me how beautiful she thinks I am. Then she kisses me. She kisses me soft and slow. Her fingers read my face like its Braille.

"You are so beautiful… Di". The way she says my name makes me wetter than I am already. She kisses my eyelids. Her lips embrace my skin's warmth, soothing, exciting makes my heart rate speed up and slow down all at the same time. She whispers in my ear as if we are not alone but in the midst of a crowded room, the words "I've wanted you since the first time I laid my eyes on you." I inhale soft and long, feel the root of my existence enter my body filling my lungs completely as she runs her hand down my thin front patch over my swollen clit letting her finger curve underneath it and make entry into my soul's desire. She moves it in and out in a circular motion as if she's trying to turn my wetness into a slow churn cream. My walls hold on to her finger with a grasp as tight as the one my thighs have on her hand and wrist.

"Yeah give me that pussy baby" her words are the opposite of her daily vocabulary driving me insane yet making me saner then I have ever been. I have a bit of difficulty allowing the width of her other two fingers inside me. I take in a short breath of surprise and brace my hands against her wrist and front thigh… my way of saying… easy baby without saying the words, as she raises my leg with her other hand. She pushes them so deep inside of me that I let out a sigh of pleasure and pain "Aah". That told her that I had not been sleeping with Vance in a while. Ramona kisses me taking in my full lip with intensity then she says,

"Work that shit for me! Work it…like you clearly don't work it for him…" Ramona watches my supple hips for a while before she takes my left breast into her mouth hungrily, releasing it only to devour the mixture of sweat and skin on my neck. She moves passionately and strong inside my core.

"Ooh… my… GOD…" I call out as she picks up her pace to a steady speed… palms my bottom… pulls me open further… I hold on to her as the room spins uncontrollably along with the sensation and my emotions. I have been with many women but none of them made me feel this way. None of them asking of me entirely. None of them causing me to cut Vance off sexually like I have and never have I slept with any one while in a relationship with him.

"Let me have you" that request made me tremble.

"Ooh… baby… Ooh…" I moan.

"Say it again!"

"What?" I question.

"Baby… Call me baby" She orders and I willingly oblige. I run my French manicured nails along her back and called her baby. She drives her fingers to their fullest length and then some then back to the tips. I gasp. She moves her body like she is wearing a strap and is slow fucking me.

"Ooh…Baby… Ooh…"My legs began to shake like leaves on a tree in the midst of the storm that's not only steering about outside but inside of me.

"Does it feel good to you?" she asks the question my body is already giving her the answer to.

" Does it feel good?" She wants me to confess with my mouth that what she is delivering is of the utmost pleasure to me. And with the persuasion of her hands movement I give in to her demand.

"Yes… Shit… yes…you feel so… fucking …good… to me!"

She pulls my hair causing me to arch my neck and my back underneath her and meet her rhythm stroke for stroke. I let out moans and sounds that I didn't know I had in me. Ramona smiles as she watches my face… examines my grinds… and synchronizes with my breathing and she cums with me. Our orgasmic sounds blend so well that, I can barely tell which ones belong to her and which belong to me. Then without warning she removes her fingers from inside me and licks and swallows all that lay within her tongues reach. I bit my lip… pull her hair… Grow from sensitivity to heightened excitement… Go from shakes to convulsions… from heavy breathing to shallow breaths. Her dark brown eyes met with my hazel ones while she licks her lips and says,

"You taste even better then I imagined you would!"

Ramona lay with her back to me as still as a statue. Knowing although the words are not spoken I am going to go. I move closer to her still no movement… I touch her, no movement… I trace her from her thigh to her neck with my fingertip…. No movement. I place my head into her back… I inhale her and feel something inside me shift… I know what she wants from me, what is required of me if I am to be in her world. I want to stay… I never wanted anything more in my life… I want to stay but I go.

Ramona Ndiaye

I toss and turn. I grab my extra-long body pillow from its place beside the one I lay my head firmly on and force it in between my thighs. I need to break the heated connection my skin is having with itself from the mere thought of her. I can't get the sounds of her breathing out of my ears… I can't escape the smell of her skin… I can't lessen her tease in my mouth no matter how many times I swallow it down… This insanity has become a reoccurring event ever since we touched. My torment started the moment she got out of my bed at the Loews hotel in New York. I ask myself you I didn't join her in her suite the second night of our layover the way she had accompanied me in mine the night before but my reasoning is what has been keeping me up at night. God knows I wanted to more than anything I've ever wanted to do in my life. I refrained from doing so because Dianah kept herself locked away like she was afraid to face me after crossing the lines of business partners and friends and. I understood that she was dealing with the reality of our actions, and even aware that she would probably be dealing with feelings that accompany infidelity. It's funny how life works sometimes when we are true to ourselves and who we are we become fallacies to others' versions of who we are or who we should be in their eyes. So I gave her space to let her work things out about who and what she wants in her life. But with all sincerity I hope that the time she is taking leads her heart to me. I feel like all I have been doing lately is thinking, praying, and longing. I'm at the point where I want to just stop into her office unannounced, just so she has to face me. I have never been the woman that has given her body and soul to someone then been dismissed. I don't know how to be this woman. I don't understand how she could walk away from me cold turkey! Our relationship is not supposed to be like this. It's five o'clock in the morning and I'm wondering about the way I make her feel. Thinking about how I want to make her feel in every way if only she would let me. I look at the clock and rub my head, how could she not care about the way I feel? I get out of the bed that feels so empty to me now, grab my cordless phone from its base, and walk into the kitchen. I dial Dianah's number as I lean on the counter she placed here as though it would bring me closer to her.

"Ramona, are you ok?" Dianah answers before the first ring ends. Her voice is low. I can tell I woke her from her slumber but her voice is full of genuine concern for me.

"I want you… I want you in the worst kind of way… I want you!" I feel the aching heat rush through my body and tread in the center of my heart.

"Ramona…" I listen to the change in Dianah's' voice and the muffled sounds of her shifting her body to wake up.

"I… I…I believe that I'm in love with you Dianah Marshall, and that love has me calling out your name in my dreams… And my dreams feel like a nightmare because I have to leave your side when I wake." My heart is pounding so hard that I feel each thumb in my throat as I await her reply.

"When I got back I tried to take my mind off of you, off of us together. I even had to leave the office a few times because so much of you already exist in my life there. I have never been a cheater, so my guilt caused me to try and refocus my attention on him, but I couldn't and I can't because all I think about is you… I… want you too… you know that." I hear her voice crack when she says the words I want you, to me and I can tell she's crying.

"I don't want to cause you any pain Dianah… I just want to love you." I say through the burn in my throat. Because my mind replays the words she once said to me "wanting something doesn't always make it so". So I swallow my burn.

"Ramona, no one has ever made me feel the way you make me feel, and every time I try to measure my feelings for you, I become unbalanced because I know that nothing or no one else can compare to you..." she says then grows silent.

"I know that you're nervous, but trust me… trust the way you feel about me… trust that I can give you all you need." I say after a few moments of silence on the line.

"I don't want you for your money." Dianah says sharply making me realize how that could have come across.

"I didn't mean it that way. My bank account is the farthest thing from my mind when I think of you… I want you… I want to be there for you in every way possible." I said quickly to make sure she knows that I don't see her as a woman that has set her sights on my finances nor am I a woman that is set on purchasing the next beautiful piece of art.

"The idea of love... loving a woman… there are no certainties…" Dianah softly speaks.

"No one knows the certainty of love until they are wrapped in it." I feel as my own tears build.

"You always speak as if life with you is so easy, so possible." I can tell that she is still struggling with the idea of my need to have her completely… Still struggling with the struggle every lesbian has had to overcome… The reality that there is never a line dividing their sexuality only one dividing judgment and non-judgment!

"It can be and I want to prove it to you. So what are we to do now?"

Vance Hunter

"Please... Jodye... We have been through this..." I say as I slide my arm into the sleeve of my shirt and begin to button it.

"Yes we have been through this too many times before." Jodye says with an eyebrow raised over one eye.

"I love you... I am not out there sleeping with Tom, Dick, and Harry." I say without looking up as I put on my shoes on the edge of Jodye's bed.

"No, only Dianah!" Jodye sharply states.

"Jodye…"

"What? How many times have you walked out of my door, out of my life to create one with her? Only to come back to me within a month or two because her pussy's not the one you crave!" Jodye's words are bitter.

"I don't come back to you because of the got damn sex Jodye!"

"Why do you come back, because I keep opening the door right?"

"I come back because I love you!" I walk over and kiss Jodye on the cheek.

"How sweet... Sing that word in my ear the way a good mother sings lullabies to her child! Maybe I'll sleep easier tonight! I am your fool I have been for fourteen years now... all the while I remain faithful to you. I let you get out of my bed late night so that you can go fuck her in yours, so you can feel like a man on someone else's scale! My work doesn't comfort me at night no matter how much I throw myself into it to mask my loneliness when doubt about us and your love for me comes crashing in on me. Maybe I should throw in the towel and find a man that is sure about what he wants!" Jodye pulls away from me slightly.

"I'm sure about what I want... I'm here aren't I?" I take Jodye's chin into my hand.

"I'm supposed to wait in the wings for the moments that you are free to come fuck me and jump for joy... Ha... the dick is good but I'm confident that there are plenty of good lays attached to the multitude of adoring eyes that view me in the magazines and even behind the camera lenses!" Jodye's words are laced with sarcasm.

"Watch what you say to me!" I advise as I feel my possessive nature rising inside.

"Why? Fair is fair!"

"I would lose it if I knew you slept with another man, Jodye!"

"Then the pain wouldn't be as overwhelming as I watch you put on one of your shirt and ties that I always have dry-cleaned and hanging in the closet awaiting your return... button your pants... Slip your size thirteen's into your oxfords preparing to leave me... to leave me with my ass aching and my heart breaking!" I can tell that Jodye's words are filled with hurt more than resentment.

"Baby, Stop!" I walked over placed my hand on Jodye's neck and look at my lover. Jodye's eyes are a breath-taking gray that entrances me then brings me back with the length and depth of the dark lashes that are damp from tears, Which I wipe away with my thumb and smile. Jodye returns the favor and I am captivated by the smile of perfectly aligned teeth. I want to kiss my lovers lips that are light brown with a hint of red as though the thoughts in Jodye's head alone made them blush but I don't. I pull Jodye's medium frame next to me and take in Jodye's fresh scent. Next to mine Jodye's skin is that of a snowflake kissed by the sun yet protected by the wind and I want nothing more than for our love to create a new tone.

Remy Gamble

I met Jodye at a casting call. We hit it off instantly. Maybe we hit it off so well because Jodye was gorgeous and knew it, just like me. So we began to hang out. I even went out with Jodye's lover that looks more like our personal bodyguard a few times. And I'll be damned, Hush, the club I was first introduced to Jodye's lover at, is the right name in this situation because all the time we've been partying, heavenly chocolate, Jodye's chosen nickname has been living a double life. Boy, how the cookie crumbles. I would've never known, seeing as she keeps that side of her life so secretive and separate. Had I not bumped into the dresser and the picture of heavenly chocolate and Dianah literally fell into my hands. Granted, had I not been fucking Ebonee in her guestroom, I would've never known. This shit is too funny finally though Miss Do Right, Be Right, 'bout to get some act right. I wonder if she knows that her secret has been keeping secrets. I think before the ringing of my cell phone breaks me away from my thoughts.

"You know you have to fix things with Ivory and Dianah right?" Chase says on the other end of the cell phone.

"Hell, Dianah was the one that forced Ebonee to tell Ivory about us. I didn't even know she walked in on me doing my thing. It's her fault shit to hit the fan because all she had to do was close the door and her mouth and no one would have been the wiser. But she couldn't do that. She had to tell my boy like that."

"Tell her like that! You can't be serious right now. You were fucking Ebonee with Ivory in the next room. That shit was foul!" Chase says.

"Don't get me wrong, I know that I crossed Ivory by hitting what was hers, but she told me, hell she told all of us that she was done with Ebonee anyway."

"That's true, but come on now, that didn't mean we could run a train on her ass and she wouldn't mind," Chase responded.

"It wasn't like I set out to do her."

"No, then tell me what it was like because I'm dying to know," Chase words are laced with curiosity.

"My feelings for Ebonee are real. She is a close friend and a good girl. Man, Ivory was dogging her and I was only trying to be a friend to Ebonee when things changed between us."

"While you were being a confidant to Ebonee what exactly where you being to Ivory when you were fucking her?" Chase questions sarcastically.

"I don't like hurting Ivory one bit. She has been down with me for years. A part of me wishes that none of this ever happened and the other part of me feels like Ivory really doesn't have a right to be mad because I'm my brother's keeper and I was just picking up her slack."

"Your brother's keeper, have you lost your ever loving mind? Chase voice went high pitched in my ear.

"I don't see how I'm the fall guy of the situation, Ivory was wrong in the way she treated Ebonee and everybody knows that. I was wrong for betraying her trust. Man, I'm not gonna say that much… I never lied to Ivory about Ebonee." I say refusing to take blame for their relationship problems.

"You never lied? What do you call fucking her behind her back?" Chase asks.

"Hell, Ivory never implied that she felt anything was even wrong with her or their relationship."

"And had she, you would have told her you were sleeping with her?"

"Man, Ivory was slippin' when she threw Ebonee away like a piece of trash. And we all know that once you discard something, it no longer belongs to you, it becomes public property," I say feeling justified.

"You need to get off that horse of yours. You didn't ride in and save a damsel in distress. You slipped your dick into forbidden pussy. Whether Ivory treated her right or not is irrelevant. You should have passed on this one. You not only fucked up a friendship that you had for years, but you disrespected and hurt a woman that was supposed to be as dear to you because you got caught in your own shit. Man up and fix it!" Chase says in an agitated tone, and then hangs up the phone in my ear.

I look at my cell in my hand and blew hot air through my lips as I flip it closed and set it down on my computer desk. I shook the mouse to wake up the PC and sat down in front of it. I login onto my messenger.

DoULike2Gamble: R u ready 2 talk 2 me now?

ThickMrs.21: Yes

DoULike2Gamble: R u ok?

ThickMrs.21: Yes

DoULike2Gamble: R u alone?

ThickMrs.21: Yes, why do you ask?

DoULike2Gamble: Then what's up with all of the one word responses?

ThickMrs.21: Because… I just don't know what to say to you :/

DoULike2Gamble: Say whatever is on ur mind. Better yet, why don't u start by telling me y u ain't answer my calls? Tell me where u been for the last 3 days.

ThickMrs.21: Remy why didn't you tell me?

DoULike2Gamble: It wasn't my place 2 tell u baby girl. Plus what a nigga look like going against my boi like that.

ThickMrs.21: I understand that but I was your lover!

DoULike2Gamble: Was? So what r u saying 2 me?

ThickMrs.21: Idk. Idk anything, anymore. I trusted you. I thought that you cared for me.

DoULike2Gamble: u know you have a piece of a nigga's heart... or I would have never ran out after ur ass 2 make sure u were ok and 2 explain…but u were ghost.

ThickMrs.21: I took a cab to get my car and some of my things before I checked in the hotel I'm staying in until I figure out my next move. Ivory and I are over. She has made that very clear on the voicemails she's been leaving on my phone.

DoULike2Gamble: So u haven't talked 2 her since the blowout?

ThickMrs.21: No. I went and picked up the rest of my things this morning and left my key while she was at work. I didn't want to do it while she was home. I knew it would just turn ugly and I don't want to fight with her anymore.

DoULike2Gamble: Where r u? I want 2 see u.

ThickMrs.21: Why do you want to see me? You don't have to feel guilty. Things between Ivory and me were over long before things between you and I began. You don't owe me anything. You can just walk away clean now.

DoULike2Gamble: And I'm not promising u anything...

ThickMrs.21: I'm in our hideaway spot... just not hiding anymore.

DoULike2Gamble: I'm on my way.

I log out, grab a few things and toss them into my duffle bag and race out the door, on my way to the La Quinta Inn. I don't know why I didn't take the out that Ebonee offered me. On the real, on most days I wouldn't have given the option much least the thought. I would have been ghost. But the things I said to Chase about Ebonee were true. Ebonee is a good girl and has always had my back. Maybe she is the one I need to complete my world. Hell, maybe I can complete hers. Everyone always says I need a sista by my side. Raven and Dianah should be proud. Chase was right; I definitely need to make things right with everybody. I will in due time, but first I have to make things right with Ebonee.

Cameron Carver

"Who knows maybe I'll see you in heaven or maybe I'll meet them in hell! No, no I don't mean that in a disrespectful manner mother. I am just saying that the saints at the church are so focused on my truth, that they don't have the time to face their own " I look over at Raven when I feel the warmth of her hand touch the skin of my fingers and squeeze them softly. Ravens arched eyebrow telling me to watch the way I speak to my mother and not just during this phone call.

"Your truth is a detestable act. Cameron, you cannot take part in the table of the Lord and the table of demons." Her words are like acid burning through me but I conceal the pain they inflect.

"Leviticus and I Corinthians, if you want to talk to me then talk to me, please don't preach at me. You have said those scripter's to me so many times that I have them memorized." I close my eyes and push the memories of her binding my demons in the name of the lord that surface to the forefront of my mind with the acknowledgment of them back to the back of my mind.

"Fine, I raised you in a house that had God as the foundation, I sent you to the best schools that money could buy, but most importantly I taught you Gods word. So I don't understand why you choose to live a homosexual life and deny God." She exhales hard.

"Deny God, how are you going to say that momma when you were there when I accepted GOD…? And I could swear with my hand on the very bible that you are throwing at me that it was your voice that blended with mine for years while I was on my knees knightly praying." I remember the warmth of my mother's palms pressing my little hands together in the center of hers as she taught me psalms 23 before tucking me in for the night.

"Cameron, accepting God is allowing your soul to bend to his will." My mothers' tone causes the warm thought to fade.

"Bending to the will of God and bending to the will of man has become so hand and hand. I'm so tired…" I let go of Ravens hand and rub my finger against my temple.

"You're tired because you are facing the attacks of the enemy without the armor of God." she is a pastor trying to save a soul.

"I'm tired of trying to explain myself to you when you don't even hear me, and honestly I don't have the time to right now. You called me just as I pulled up to an event I am speaking at tonight." I feel like this conversation and relationship is a battlefield and we are once again on opposing sides.

"Just because I don't agree with what you are saying doesn't mean that I don't hear you. Cameron, you have always had the words to bless a nation but because of your choices you allow them to be stifled." My mother's words are bitter sweet to hear.

"You don't… all you hear are the voices of your congregation and socialites'. Do you know how hard it is for me to accompany you places and act like I don't hear their whispers, see their pointing fingers, or smile while they pass me the phone numbers to their sons that I have been forcibly introduced to over the years at some function or another. And though I share no interest with or in any of them they all long to be the man that defines his manhood by entering my body and making me a real woman!" My words express my distain.

"You need to do what God has called you to do. It's time that you choose a fitting man and take your rightful place and inheritance!" I don't hear the guided tongue of God, the unconditional love of a mother, or the understanding of a woman that knows what it's like to live, love, or hurt.

"A fitting man?" I repeat her words angrily causing Raven to turn and face me with a look full of unpleasant thoughts covering her face.

"I know that you have feelings for her, but you can develop the same feelings or stronger with a nurturing man."

"I have more than feelings for Raven that's why I married her!" I don't back down.

"Not in the eyes of God, not in the eyes of the state, and definitely not in mine!" Her voice is laced with arrogance.

"Thank you for making who I am to you, ever so clear pastor." I feel the burn in my chest travel up wards until it reaches my eyes then spill over.

"Don't be condescending Cameron Caver, I only want what's best for you."

"You want to dictate my life from your planned notes, where I fall in line with your expectations, paint my face with a smile, and joining hands with the most influential candidate." My tone is low but my emotions are high.

"I want you to live your life the way you have to now, so that when your time is over on earth that you will have eternal life." Her words cause my heart to break.

"You can't take part in the table of the Lord and the table of demon's mother. It's sad that we are both filled with the love of God, but because we view him from the vision of our own eyes, we can no longer see each other. So, the time has come for us to let go." My words render my mother speechless.

In her silence, I want to tell her that I want to hear the words well done said to me by God and by her. I want to tell her that I love her more then she will ever know. I want to tell her how much I long the embrace of my mother without the judgment of her religious beliefs. I want to tell her that I pray for the day that I am only her daughter, and she is only my mother. But what good would come of saying what has been said too many times before. So instead, I say the only two words that I have never said to her.

"Goodbye mother." I press the end button on my cell.

The host of tonight's event calls out my name and I make my way to the stage. I step close to the microphone and the spotlight is turn on me. I close my eyes, inhale, and transform so I can entertain.

"She

She came to tell me that my shit was hot

That she was digging the plot

That when the words stopped

My voice did not

And she had to meet the woman whose essence reminisces between her eyes and her thighs

When she closed them

Her mellow tone

Her structured bone was now erect

And she wanted to perfect a rugged stroke with me

She wanted to perfect a rugged stroke with me

If only I would allow her to be more then

More than a boy

More than a brother

More than a friend should be

Closer to a lover

She wanted me to love her

Or at least sexually

See she wanted me to see that she was

Indeed a woman

Who desired me

And the fact that she would let go of her aggression

To lessen the impact of the connection she felt she had with me

To feel the affection of my perfected jagged stroke

Between her sheets

Had my ass a blaze in ways unimagined to me

See 'Honey' not only had the same stance but the same titles as me

Dominate

Aggressor

Daddy

Some body's Papi

Fuck

While she's Sexin

She's somebody's papi

Yet she's telling me

She wants to wrap her lips around the untamed veins of my dick

Deep

And have me fill every hole

Regardless of her pleads

Until she seeps' multiple orgasms

Courtesy of me

Leaving nothing but

Remnants on cold linen sheets"

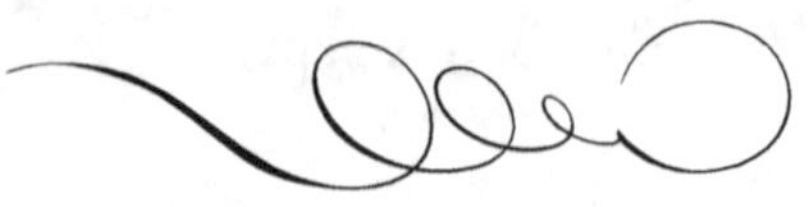

Ebonee Price

I throw the room key on the small wooden table and pile the last of the storage boxes in the corner inside my hotel room. I had to empty out my storage to average out enough money to pay for this room another month. I look around the room and take in the sight of all I own crammed into its small space. When I moved in with Ivory, she had already lived there, so everything and I do mean everything was set to her liking. Hell, even after living with her for two years not one item of furniture belonged to me. I guess if I would have really paid attention to that I would have known sooner rather than later that nothing ever would belong to me or truly be shared between us. I shake off the thoughts of my shattered happily ever after that she promised me and live in my now. I run my fingers along the soft fibers of the cocoa teddy bear that I've had since I was eighteen. I kick my shoes off and walk to the foot of the bed. I let my body fall on top of the Queen size bed that I covered with my on sheets and spread. I allow my body to give into my exhaustion from completing the daunting task of moving boxes back and forth all day. Then I feel vibrating by my knee and I reach down for my smart phone.

"Yeah..." I let out a hard breath after reading Remy's name displayed on the screen.

"Damn baby girl, it's like that now?" Remy asks in a half joking tone of voice.

"What happened this time Remy? You know you were supposed to help me get the last of my things out of storage eight o'clock this morning." I'm pissed with Remy and my tone of voice sends the message to her loud and clear.

"Pops got slammed at the shop and called me in to work."

"Whatever Remy! It's damn near eight pm now and it's a damn Sunday!" I yell into the phone, close my eyes, and rub my hands across my forehead.

"Come on baby girl. Don't be like that. I'm gonna make it up to you ma." She says in the voice that I used to think was cute but have come to know that it's just a prelude to another one of her lies. I'm so not feeling her lies right now, so I call her on her mounting broken promises.

"Like the way you gonna make up to me not being able to help me with the money to move into my own place when I asked you for help or how you gonna make up to me not having the five hundred dollars that you promised to give back to me if I let you borrow it." I'm so fed up with her and her lies. I can't believe I believed her when she told me that she would be here for me.

"Damn, ma you making a nigga feel like shit when I was just calling to kick it with you."

"I'll pass. I have been moving heavy ass boxes by myself all day. I'm fucking exhausted and I have to go into work early tomorrow. I'm sure you will find someone else to kick it with tonight." I end the call on her and throw the phone across the bed. I feel myself becoming emotional and I'm way too exhausted to be up all night thinking about how or what I need to do to get my life on track.

RAVEN WINTERS-CARVER

The tone in Dianah's voice when she called me earlier this morning, while I was parking outside of my office building, asking me to come by to see her after work had my mind running wild all day. I hope everything went okay with the new company. I know how hard she worked to make this happen. So I cut my work day short, only seeing two patients, and headed over to her place. 'It's a good thing that I did because I can tell that she's been crying as soon as she opens the door.

"When I look at her, my heart trembles and I lose track of all that was in my mind before her. And I don't want to look forward to the future thoughts that are to form in my mind if they are not of her… She has me… She has me captive in her essence." Dianah says as she paces back and forth in front of me in her living room.

"Ramona?" I ask instinctively with a smile and ease up to the edge of the cushion on the couch I'm sitting on.

"Please don't judge me Ray," she says with her face turned away from me so when she completes her paced turn and looks at me, I expect her look to match the one I was giving her that read… Girl, I know you didn't just go there with me… but instead her eyes are filled with tears. I take her hand and pull her closer to me as I stand up and get closer to her. I look at her flushed face that's beginning to redden under her eyes and on the top of her nose. I feel the tears fill up then spill out of my own eyes as my soul connects with my friend's emotions.

"Dianah, talk to me." I ease my shoulder from under her wet cheek, then guide her to the couch. We both let our bodies sink into the cushions at the same time. Dianah wipes away her tears with the soft fabric of her sweater's sleeve, then she fingers her bottom lip nervously for a few minutes before she starts to let out what's got her in this state.

"I have never done them both at the same time." She looks at me then lowers her head so that her eyes fall away from mine. Because even though her words came out strained like that of a speech therapy patient, I hear what she's saying to me clearly. I know her as well as she knows me and she knows that I know what she is trying to tell me but I don't jump the gun. I anxiously wait for her to get the rest of her words together.

"Her skin glows… and her scent is so deep into my senses that even from across a room full of multiple blends of cologne, I smell it as though she was standing right next to me… her eyes pierced my soul with each glance she gave me. Her voice, oh my God, her voice sends chills down my spine and heat through my veins." Dianah places her hand close to her chest as though she was filing the heat just reminiscing about it and it causes her to get up and start her pace again. This time she moves slow, runs her fingers through the loose ends of her hair that's hanging freely from her ponytail.

"I did my best to keep my distance from her in the weeks before our meeting in New York, because she made her feelings and desires clear to me." She tries to bring rationale where there is none.

"Which are?" I question as though I don't remember the conversation we had prior about Ramona's interest in her.

"Her desire is to have me in her life full time, she wants to love me freely, and she wants me to give myself to her completely!" Dianah says as she looks at me nervously.

"And that scares the hell out of you doesn't it?" I say as I lean back on the couch. I shake my head slightly with a half-smile because we both know it does.

"After spending all day in the board room and getting checked into my hotel suite because of the snow storm, I was in no mood to sit down and eat in a crowded restaurant. So when Ramona suggested we share a quiet dinner for two in her suite, I was all for it." Dianah says as though she didn't just bypass my question.

"You're not as slick as you think you are!" I joke and she lets out a giggle before she sits back down next to me and tucks her feet under her knees as she sits Indian style.

"We ate and fed each other from off one another's plates at times, both of us wanting the other to know exactly what we were experiencing in flavors." She attempts to explain the intimacy shared between them.

"Ah huh…"

"I could tell that she wanted me just as much as I had been longing her, even though I didn't show her. I wanted her so much that I had to stay away from her in fear that I would have to make her mine."

"D, I've never heard you talk about anyone like this before." I say completely intrigued by her acknowledgement of her true feelings for Ramona.

"That's because I have never felt this way before Ray… I want to have her and let her have me in every way imaginable."

"In every way?" I cut my eye at her knowing that throughout her years of dealings with women she always kept a strict no strapping rule. And whenever I ask her why she won't let a woman do that to her she would always give me her simplified reasoning which was that's what she has Vance for.

"Girl, in every way!" she answers promptly.

I look at Dianah and remain still to see if she is pulling my leg. After a few minutes of silence I know she is serious.

"Ramona moved in close to me. I could feel the heat of her skin ricochet off of mine as she pushed me up against the wall with her body and took my bottom lip into her mouth for the first time." Dianah rubs her finger slowly along her lips and keeps going.

"Ramona made me hotter than I have ever been and as terrified in the same moment… the shivers through my body told her how much I wanted her. As my mind told me that I was in a relationship with Vance and that all the things my body was crying out for would be wrong if I let them happen… even though I had stopped sleeping with Vance three months prior."

"Really why did you?" I ask with question in my eyes that ask her if he had done something to cause her to do stop.

"When I was with him, I couldn't get Ramona out of my head. When he touched me, his hands weren't hers… I was in a relationship with him but I felt like in every moment I spent with him I was cheating on her," Dianah says looking to me for understanding in the emotions she's been going through.

"I tried to fight my desire for her touch. I even brought up Vance… trying to remind Ramona and myself that I was not free to indulge!"

"I take it that it wasn't the buzz kill you'd hoped for?"

"Hell no… she looked at me with such intensity, then kissed me with passion that I can't measure if I tried to." She shook her head side to side and grabbed a throw pillow and placed it between her legs.

"I don't remember what came off first or last. I just know that she moved things inside me that I though belonged where they were, and placed them with new things… made room for new feelings, a new longing… new possibilities." She smiles and I do too.

"You made love to her, Dianah."

"And she made love to me. She was more than I thought she'd be."

"I can attest to that just off of what you told me about her since the art show."

"Raven, I was lying in bed with her after we were done and it felt right."

"What felt right?" I dig to see if she is ready to say the very words she has fought her whole life."

"Her next to me… Ramona's naked skin against mine… It felt right and for the first time in my life I could not only see myself waking up to her every morning and falling asleep in her arms every night, but I wanted to. Then reality set in and I knew the only way I could have that with her is by giving her all of me like she asked me to. But I didn't have all of me to give, not in that moment. I was still Vance's woman and he was my man. And I after what we had done I was a cheater." Her eyes began to water again.

"Awe D." I say taking her hand into mines.

"How would she see me now? Would she think that I was a woman that gave into my desires at will? That I would cheat on her if we got together like I have just done with her… I was open for her and ashamed at myself for doing what I did as pleasurable as it was…" she wipes her tears.

"Dianah, you guys have been battling emotions for each other for almost a year now. I seriously doubt that she would think of you as a loose woman." I say with a strong face.

"Really Ray?" Dianah questions my opinion.

"Really Dianah … so when are you going to tell her that you have fallen in love with her?"

"I'm gonna tell her as soon as I end things with Vance once and for all."

"You mean you are getting rid of your blankie?" I laugh and she bumps into me and laughs a bite too.

"I don't need Vance anymore. Honestly Ray, I feel safer in Ramona's presence than I ever felt wrapped in his arms!"

"Are you saying what I think you're saying?"

"I'm saying I want to be in her world and if I have to give her all of me, then that's what I will give."

"I'm so proud of you Dianah!" I say as I squeeze her in my arms and kiss her face, that even though is red and swollen, has a glow of love on it.

"I love you too, Ray. But I can't breathe."

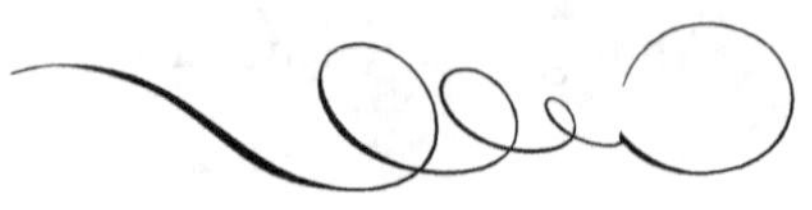

Ivory Dinero

I lay the hand written letter that Remy left for me at my front door down by the long steam yellow rose that came attached to it. I exhale hard and think back to the day I told her the meaning of its color, and the symbolization of its thorns. We both know the game, hell we often played it well together. I know that two wrongs don't make ah wright so I don't blame Ebonee for doing to me what I did to her. If it had been any other woman Ebonee cheated on me with I could chock it up to the game, but the shit cuts deep because Remy was my best friend. Over the years Remy and I have been through thick and thin together. I never thought that my boy would be my true enemy. I feel the burn in my chest rise and sting my eyes causing them to water. The more I think about how I was the one that always came through for her when all her so called friends would let her down, the more I cry. I lay my head in the palm of my hands and wonder if I should believe the words of apology that Remy put in this letter.

I hear my cell going off in the bedroom. I wipe away the fallen tears from my eyes but before I have the chance to get up off of my sofa to get it, I hear my bedroom door open followed by footsteps that lead to me.

"Who's calling you at one o'clock in the morning Ivory? Fantasy questions as she hands me my cell then stands there in one of my white T's with her arms folded and one eye brawl raised watching me.

"Hello… What…And how in the hell did that happen Paul? No, no that will fry the system. Listen to me and listen carefully. You have to go to the main frame and pull the hard ware." I look at fantasy and see the expression on her face soften now that she realizes that it's someone from my job.

"Sorry." She mouths the word and shifts her weight to her other foot.

"Ok. Where you able to retrieve it? Thanks what you are supposed to see. Yeah. Make sure that you back it up this time. I hang up the phone and place it on the couch next to me and she waste no time moving her body in front of me.

"I didn't know that it was work related." Fantasy says as she kisses me on my neck softly. "You know I have to keep my eye on you."

"Is that right?" I ask her as I run my hand over her round bottom.

"Yes." She replies teasingly before she looks at the letter and the rose on my coffee table and turns her lips up. Fantasy pushes them off of the table on to the floor.

"Now why you gonna act like that?" I give her a look that says what's up with that.

"You need to stop reading that shit. I have something better for you to place your focus on." Fantasy says then lays her back on the glass and opens her legs. She displays the shaven lips between her thighs then she moves her finger in the come hither motion. I bend my back and place my head in between her thighs. I run my tongue from her bottom whole to the top one.

"Mmm, yeah daddy, lick my shit just like." Fantasy says while she caresses the back of my head with one of her hands and caressing and sucking on her left breast with the other.

I keep licking and sucking her long and slow. I make her dig her nails into my shoulders from the build of sensation. She works her bottom with my tongue, lets her head hang over the side of the table, and lets out a moan after moan.

"Make me cum. Yes make me fucking cum all down your throat!" she orders picking up her pace causing me to do the same until the muscles in her body tense and she cums in my mouth.

"Damn." She says when I release the suction I had on her still swollen clit.

"It feels good baby?"

"Hell yeah, and you know that that just made me horny." She tells me what I already know.

I stand up, take her hand, and lead her to the bedroom to finish what I started.

A Picture's Worth A Thousand Words

"If I ask you to trust me on all things could you do it? If I need you to map your position would you try it? You constantly talking 'bout how much you love me, want me, need me, Show me stop talking no more conversation necessary!" I sing along with the sound of the Jill Scott CD thumbing through the surround sound speakers that fills every room in my house. I inhale the fragrance of laughter that fills the air tonight. The fogged table has its usual two decks of cards, one red and white and the other blue and white, in the center. Neither deck has been opened yet. But it seems that cards aren't the thing tonight. No, tonight is not about the playful boasting, shit talking, and spankings with each slap of the card as it hits the glass or the tongue lashes to egos that fight to gain leverage. Tonight each glance of the eye, each curve of a smile, each nod of the head, each unconscious touch that brushes ones knee, thigh, shoulder, or hand will mend the damaged areas of friendships that life sometimes brings. Yes, each action will form a connection that will reinforce the depth of willed understanding given to and from imperfect souls. Form a connection beautiful in its existence alone that illuminates the strength and love of friendship through the power of forgiveness.

I look across the living room and allow my eyes to make me a voyeur as they boldly settle in on my lover's lips and I watch them part, then reconnect intensely as she partakes in a riled debate with Cameron and Ivory about whether or not the Miami Heat's dream team, that consists of Dewayne Wade, Chris Bosh, and LeBron James, are going to take the team to the playoffs. Chase feels the heat of my eyes on her and stops speaking long enough to brandish a smile at me. I lick my lips and do the same to her before my eyes move on. I admire the glow that gleams off of Dianah's face now that she has come into her true self as she tilts her head back with an open mouthed laugh. I'm not sure what Jodye said, but it has Raven holding her chest like she's trying to control her laughter long enough to take in a breath. I'm glad that Jodye seems to have fit right in, because men and women are usually on opposite ends of the spectrum, family or not. And that was one of my concerns when Remy asked me if she could bring one of her friends and cast members along tonight, because she was coming straight from a shoot and it was her turn to drive in their car pool. The other was the fact that tonight is the first night that we are all face to face with one another since the blow out at Dianah's, where Remy and Ivory came to blows after Dianah walked in on Remy sexing Ebonee. Don't get me wrong, we have all talked on the phone or met up in what I like to call "comfort groups". Comfort groups are those of us that feel a little more comfortable talking to each other be it because we have known each other longer or share the same state of mind such as a feminine or dominate woman. And Remy has made her rounds apologizing in the circle of friends. She had beautiful flower arrangements sent to Raven and Dianah's offices and one sent to the ER for me. Remy made sure that all the arrangements were personalized so that we could see and feel the sincerity in her gesture. Remy took Cameron and Chase out for drinks, on her. Remy extended the invitation to Ivory as well, but the wound of Remy's betrayal was too fresh and Ivory wasn't quite ready to make amends so she declined her invite. I overheard Cameron fussing with Chase earlier this evening about the fact that it wasn't the letter that Remy left at Ivory's baring her soul but that it was the single long stemmed yellow rose that Remy placed on her doorstep every morning for the past two months that finally chipped away the ice from Ivory's broken heart and brought Ivory here tonight to face her estranged friend. I close my eyes and lightly shake off the negative energy of such a betrayal. I open my eyes just in time to witness Remy enter the living room from the kitchen with a bottle of beer in one hand and a red cup in the other. Remy walks over and hands the cup to Jodye, then takes a seat on the chaise that is directly in between both conversations and sipped her beer.

"This is delicious!" Jodye says as his hand grips the plastic red cup full of wine punch that has pieces of liquor soaked fruit at the bottom and takes another sip.

"Be careful now. It's easy going down but it will have you gone before you know it!" Dianah says and we all start laughing thinking about how many times we have found ourselves toasted from the very same drink.

"So Jodye, how long have you been acting?" I ask as I sit down in the empty space next to him.

"I've only been taking on roles for about two years now." He answers without reserve.

"Really. What did you do before hand, if I may ask?" Raven inquires trying to learn more about him as well.

"I have been modeling for department stores and magazines since I was 19." Jodye says in a modest tone.

"I can defiantly see you doing that and remaining a top pick!" I say with a smile because he is a very attractive man by his features along but add his naturally gray eyes and he is stunning.

"I second that, you are a gorgeous man." Dianah agrees with me as she openly admired his features. Raven and I join her along with everyone else with eyes in the room.

"Thank you ladies, and yes I do remain desirable as far as work is concerned. Unfortunately, on a personal note my looks nor am I enough for the one man that I want to desire me, the way other people in the world do." Jodye shrugs his shoulders.

Jodye's words are honest and full of hurt that he chases with a few swallows of wine punch, I assume try to stop the ache in his heart. The weight of his words causes Chase, Ivory, Cameron and Remy to grab their drinks and join in the open conversation.

"Then he is a foolish man, because in the short time that I've spent with you tonight, you have been nothing but sincere. So I am going to assume that you are just as open with your lover as you have been with us tonight." I say with compassion.

"I think that I have been too open, too accepting of the things that he said he needed in his life…" Jodye says as though he is reevaluating his past actions with his lover.

"Being open and honest with your partner about the things he needs is important but did you ever tell him what it is that you need, want, and expect from him? Because sometimes they are truly unaware of the things their significant others desire… after all a person can only treat you the way you allow them to!" Raven says in a direct yet comforting tone.

"Raven, you're right. He has only done to me what I have allowed him to do to me…I should have put my foot down alone time ago… Now I'm in love with a man that lives his life undercover. Yet we have lived together so many times throughout the fourteen years we have been together, that any state would deem us common-law partners and we would be equally dividing up properties. Now that he thinks he has to leave me, what we shared completely in order to obtain another, when she doesn't even know him!" Jodye looks up with watered eyes to receive what I'm sure he felt would be judgment or contempt for what he just confessed to strangers but was eating him up inside.

"Fourteen years says a lot, granted that's a long time to go through the stage of uncertainty about who you are. And I'm in no way passing judgment. I do understand that it's not as easy for a man to live openly even in today's society. But years and property that man loves you even if he is too blind to see it." Cameron shakes her head with a smile.

"Love damn sure makes a bitch blind to the things you don't want to see." Remy says in a sarcastic and insensitive tone.

"Not blind, but definitely foolish to think that love guaranties loyalty. " Ivory replies in a sharp but controlled tone. We all know that Remy's words strike a nerve.

"As painful as his choice has been, you still love him don't you?" Chase question forces Jodye to admit what we all see and takes the focus off of Remy's stupidity.

"I guess I am a fool for him, always have been" He says as he wipes away the tears that he has been trying to keep from falling all night. Jodye takes out a picture of his undercover lover and hands it to Chase.

"Damn… He's huge!" Chase says causing Raven that was sitting next to her to lean in and sneak a peek before it made its way to her.

Raven's eyes squint, then her mouth drops open. I can tell by her facial expression that something was seriously wrong. I waste no time making my way to her side to see what was captured in that picture. I feel a wave of heat flood my body as I see what has rendered Raven speechless. But before either of us has time to warn our friend, she is blind-sided just as we have been. Dianah takes in an empty breath as she holds onto the image of Jodye and Vance posed in a loving embrace and time stands still.

Dianah Marshall

I take in the image of Vance and Jodye... I take in their closeness... I take in the familiar way Jodye's hand lays over Vance's muscular arm... I take in the way Jodye's slender but tone body rest relaxed against Vance's broad chest... I take in their smiles... their... smiles are so real.

"Jodye..." I whisper the name as my heart pumps used oxygen to my brain. In my mind I flash to the time I was in bed with Vance and he called out his name while he was inside of me. I thought Jodye was an insignificant woman that Vance had relations with in my absence. "I'm gonna cum so fucking hard Jodye!" His words chill my spine and I go numb. This truth is so raw, I taste blood.

"Dian..." I hear half my name come out of Kioni's mouth before I snap.

"Fuck this shit!" I flick the wallet size photo at Jodye, and it hits him in his chest before it tumbles to his lap causing his emotion to change instantly.

"What's going on?" Chase asks the question I'm sure was running through every one's minds except Raven and Kioni's, because they are the only ones that I share any aspect of Vance with.

"The undercover brother that Jodye is so in love with is the same man, hell the only man that Dianah has been in a relationship with." Raven's words echo in my ears while filling everyone in on what Vance was keeping from me and I was keeping from them.

"What?" Chase yells looking at Kioni then zoning in on Jodye.

"This is Vance?" Cameron examines the picture that she picks up off the floor.

"You're Dianah?" Jodye says as his puzzled eyes lock in on me. He is doing the same thing I am doing to him, sizing him up, comparing our similarities, and then discarding them in the same moment. He is no longer a welcomed member of our social pride family. He is a thief that has eased his way into my temple that I left unguarded. But will fight to the death to defend.

"Dianah!" Ivory calls out and begins to make her way over to me, as she sees my fingers curl into fists at my sides.

"I can tell that this is just as unexpected for you as it is for me but I'm sure we can handle this like two adults, right?" Jodye stands from his once seated position and readjust his clothes.

"Damn Dianah, you sure know how to pick 'em! " Remy says as she sits up in her seat with a smirk and takes a sip of her beer like she is enjoying this moment.

I cut my eyes at Remy before refocusing them on Jodye who is also locked in on Remy. Jodye and I realize that we are both ponds for the second time around. I hold up my finger and say "one minute... wait just one minute." I turn and walk to the kitchen. I'm nauseous at the thought of Jodye and Vance together. Nauseous because of the things I have done for Vance sexually. Things I didn't really enjoy, but I knew made him feel good. I wanted to make him feel good. He was my man. I feel the walls spin as I reach the center of the kitchen. I run to the sink, grip the rim and bring up the knots in my stomach.

"Awww sweetie..." Raven says as she lifts the faucet and lets the water push my vomit down the drain while Kioni gathers my hair in her hands taking it out of my face.

"It's gonna be ok..." Kioni says just before I hear Jodye's damn voice from the other side of the kitchen.

"I really didn't know that I was talking with the infamous Dianah... bearing my soul if you will. Just so you know, I did tell Vance to tell you the truth about his sexuality when I found out things had become sexual between you and him... As you see my opinion doesn't weigh much when it comes to what part you fill in his life... But now that I know who you are and you know who I am... It's only fair that you tell me one thing..." Jodye pauses a moment then says "Have you truly let him go this time or is this just another one of your fish binges?"

I inhaled his words and exhaled fury, because they tell me that I have been the fucking topic of their discussions, yet I knew nothing of Jodye. I hate to admit it but at this point I realize that Vance has not only been pulling the wool over Jodye's eyes but he has pulled the wool over mines as well. I have spent over ten years of my life with Vance and I don't know him. I feel my heart speed up then I feel it slow down, along with time, and my actions are in slow motion. I grab one of the cutting knives from the wooden knife block on the counter next to me. I throw it at Jodye. I aim for his heart but he moves and it breaks skin on his left shoulder instead.

"Bitch, you done lost your fucking mind!" Jodye grabs the large bowl of wine punch and tosses it at me. It hits me dead in my chest and the liquid cools the sting of its impact as it covers me. Before Chase, Cameron, Ivory and Remy could make their way into the kitchen to stop either of our assaults towards each other...

"Hell naw, it ain't even going down like this podnaah!" Cameron says as she runs over and stands in front of me with Ivory at her side.

"Since the two of you talk about me... I'm sure Vance told you that he begged me not to end our relationship completely and walks out of his life... No, huh... I'm not surprised that he didn't share the details on how your heart ache is his symbol of love to me... or the measures I had to take to get him to leave my house that night…" I tell him things that he doesn't know and watch him wrestle with hurt and pain.

"Stay the fuck away from my man!" Jodye replies the only way he can and that's with anger.

"Your man?" I laugh. "When you are sucking his dick you are licking my pussy! How do you like my taste?" My words were as poisonous to his ears as his have been to mine. Jodye's eyes dim and he stands stunned, long enough to digest the idea.

"I would tell you to kiss my ass Dianah but that would be a step down from the dry juices you've been swallowing!" His tempter and tongue are parallel to mine as he tries to get closer to me.

His words pierce my soul. We both know that we just put a face to one another but through Vance's lying deceitful actions we are not strangers to each other.

"It's time for you to go." Chase says as she walks toward him just as Remy began to half heartily help Chase try to get the situation under control.
"Come on Jodye, man let's bounce." Remy says as she pulls at Jodye's wounded left arm and out of nowhere, Jodye turns his rage onto her. Jodye hits Remy with a right handed haymaker. The blow is so hard that it takes Remy clean off of her feet. Remy lands on top of the table with the food spread. The weight of her body sends plates flying as she breaks the table and falls to the floor.

"Did you think I was gonna let the fact that you brought me here slide? You have been out with us, smiling and laughing in my damn face knowing she was fucking him!" Jodye says as he kicks Remy in her side while she is still down.

"That's enough, it's time for you to go." Chase says as she uses her training locking her arms under Jodye's and pressing her hands on the back of his neck to take control of Jodye once and for all. Cameron assist Chase in getting him out of the house. I could hear Jodye yelling profanities the whole way.

I walk over to Remy while she's gripping her side there on the floor covered in food we were enjoying just an hour ago and pick up the beer bottle on the counter, then empty the half full bottle onto Remy's head. She wrenches as the alcohol runs across the open flesh on her face mixing with blood. "I hope it burns like hell, you trifling, good for nothing, type of something!"

"You are no longer welcome in my home. Get this fucking trash out of my house." Kioni says as she looks at Chase and Cameron as they make their way back to the kitchen.

"Gladly, I'm so tire of her and her fucking hoe games!" Cameron says and waste no time in grabbing Remy up by one arm and Chase by the other.

"To think that you meant the shit you said in that fucking letter…. You are never gonna change… you are a piece of shit!" Ivory says as she grabs Remy's legs.

" I can't believe you had a fucking hand in this, you will truly get what's coming to you." Raven says as she follows them as they carry Remy through the living room, then practically drops Remy to the ground a few feet away from the front door.

Vance Hunter

I am jolted out of my sleep by the ice of the cold water that smacks my face while drenching my chest and sheets before soaking into the mattress. "What the fuck!" I franticly question as my heart pounds in my throat and I open my eyes to find Jodye standing over me with an empty bucket in hand.

"I'm facing your lies and swallowing my bitter truth, I'm tired of reaching out for you when you are already gone." Jodye says as he throws the bucket at me. I feel my anger change the temperature of my chilled skin as I sling the wet blanket off of me sending the bucket crashing to the floor on the other side of the bed and jump to my feet landing in front of him in what seemed like one motion.

"What the fuck are you talking about?" I wipe away the last bit of my drowsiness with the draining water that covered my face.

"I'm talking about trying to be all you need me to be for years and how you have the fucking balls to say you want her above me!"

"If you are so fucking tired, then what the hell are you doing here when I already told you what I want?" I'm enraged with Jodye and myself for not taking back my key when I told him that I wanted to make things work with Dianah.

"You want a normal life so I'm a fucking sacrifice… an offering that you lay at her fucking feet to win her got damn heart… How dare you fucking trample on mine in the process…? Like all the years I put into you, us, this relationship means nothing!" Jodye sharply responds. His gray eyes are filled with a rage that I have never seen before. I hear the air as it passes my ear, next I feel the blow land on the left side of my face unexpectedly causing me to shift in my stance a bit before the next two connect with my head. I grab his wrest in midair and hit him with a right of my own that sends him to the floor hard. Jodye grabs his face, balls into a fetal position and begins to rock with pain.

"Oh shit, baby, I didn't mean to…" I drop down on one knee to check on Jodye but when I reach out to touch him he scurries away from me holding his left hand up as a guard to keep me at bay and I notice for the first time the blood trail dripping from a make shift bandage on his arm and I realize that not only has he been drinking but he has gotten into it with someone else before me tonight as well.

"You hit me… I can't believe you actually hit me…" Jodye mumble's, shakes his head back and forth as though he is fighting back his disbelief of my action as the tears stream his face that is already starting to swell and change into a reddish color around his eye.

"Come on Jodye… Don't act like you didn't just swing on me, I hit you out of reflex…" I cover my mouth with the palm of my hand full of regret as I rub my jaw and watch the physical and emotional pain flow down Jodye's face.

"Looking at things now, it was silly of me to have spent all those nights alone… while you spent those same nights fucking her to feel like you were a real man… Huh… while all I got in return was the warm embraces of your forbidden love that you only express to me behind closed doors or at Hush… that would leave me to wonder what it was that she had to make you choose her over me, when I gave you all of me… Gave you my heart, my soul, my mind, my acceptance of who I thought you were. I even gave you my got damn emotion and even hated her for you, every time her leaving you for a woman would strike a blow to your fucking ego… But meeting her tonight… having to face the fact that she owns part of me is way too much to for my heart to handle!" Jodie cuts his eyes at me as he pulls himself up off the wooden floor.

"What do you mean you meeting her?" I question as a sharp pain runs through my heart as the words 'meeting her' replay in my mind at the idea his words imply. I have always made sure to keep them and remnants of them away from each other so that they would never know each other if their paths ever happen to cross, which was highly unlikely.

"She's a very attractive woman." Jodye continues talking as though he didn't hear my question.

"You both are!" I snap showing my agitation with his desperate attempt to raddle me.

"I admit that I played my part in letting things get to where they are between you and her but I was here first... I Thought been open to you being with her would make you happy... So why it's me that you feel deserves the pain of your rejection, I'll never understand... I've always been faithful to you, unlike her... You are also my first and only Vance, So why her? "He whips at the tears that fall from his right eye with the back of his right hand.

Jodye's words reveal facts that up until now only I knew about my position in both relationships, he's not bluffing.

"Oh my God..." I clinch my chest over the area that my heart usually beats strong and feel no rhythm. Thoughts of what Dianah must be thinking of me right now are racing through my mind a million miles a minute and I feel the panic of her knowing running ramped inside me.

"Yes, Dianah knows all about the dirty little secret that you have been keeping!" His tone is somewhere in between sadness and relief.

"I don't know how the two of you... Jodye, I need to know exactly what you told her... What did you tell her? What did you tell her about us?" My words are full of fear and desperation and my lover knows it, he knows me, and lashes out.

"What I told Dianah? You should be asking me what it is that she told me... and that's everything! How you so easily sacrificed what we shared for well over your precious ten years off and on with her… even after she told you she had moved on!" Jodye looks at me with piercing eyes like it's the first time he ever truly saw me and walks with speed out of the bedroom heading for the door.

"Wait it wasn't like that. I love you; you know that but I'm just not like you, Jodye… I'm not gay!" I tell him the same thing I told myself when we move in together for the first time, again when we walked the streets of Amsterdam on one of our annually vacations together, and when I put in half the founds on the house that he lives in and holds my clothes, items, and memories of the life we share together.

"Love me, you had my heart in your hands and you let it fall violently to the ground!" Jodye says as he pulls his arm away from me and picks up his keys and quickly removes his key to the condo from the key ring.

"Jodye, don't do that… please let me…" I try to explain but he cuts me off mid sentence.

"Do you remember when I brought you this place?" he smiles as he looks around the condo.

"Yes, of course I do. You told me that you loved me enough to let me have both worlds!" Repeating the words he said to me years ago bring me to tears because they force me to face the depth of the love I know Jodye has for me.

"How foolish was I to ever think that I could have it all?" I lower my head because the last thing I wanted to do was cause either of them pain.

"No more compromises!" Jodye places the key on the edge of the accent table and walks out the door.

I watch the door close behind the only person in the world that truly knows me and I have never felt more alone.

Cameron Carver

I'm sitting on the left side of Dianah, Raven is setting on her right. I feel the cold of the hard plastic collide with the elevated heat of my body temperature. Dianah's fear and tears are an instant reflection of my life… of me… more than a decade ago. That's why I was adamant that we drive an hour and a half to the 84th street clinic in Broward County, away from where she lives and her regular physician is located. Her health insurance would cover the cost but not the embarrassment of having to inform them of every one of her sexual partners of the last ten years… of Vance's sex escapades that landed her in need of every STD testing available.

Dianah's body shakes nervously as Raven wipes away the tears falling from Dianah's right eye and kisses her cheek softly.

"How could I have been so naive?" Dianah asks shaking her head from side to side. She is clearly pushing back every memory that enters her thoughts.

"Not naïve Di, naïve would have been going against your instincts and sexing him without protecting yourself!" Raven comforts her best friend.

"But Raven… how good is using that protection when I did other things without using any? Not often but I did… how did I not see what was right in front of me? Dianah's voice sounds to be weakened by the truth.

I take her free hand into mine and say "The same way I didn't see what was in front of me." My voice is low but loud enough. Dianah looks at me, then at Raven, then back at me.

"Loveless… her name was Loveless." The events of my past plays in my mind as I tell them through my mouth.

"I had this feeling I did not understand when I passed him by the stairs and he nodded to say what's up. I replied with a slight hello as I kept it moving. I made it to the parking lot of my building and my legs were no longer moving forward, they only allowed me to go in reverse. I didn't want to think that he was waiting for my disappearance to make his appearance. I found myself turning the key all the while telling myself this can't be, yet I walked in smelling the air, entered the bedroom, our room, their room in that moment. That moment that my eyes witnessed her chocolate legs open with his bare ass striding, with his jeans down around his ankles between them, and each of his hands palming the bottom of what was promised exclusively to me, as naked as my heart's beat, now both being braced against a wall. Her eyes closed, mouth half open exhaling ecstasy as she pressed her dark face against his muscular high yellow shoulder and neck. He panted with a rhythm of a boxer pounding away at his opponent. Her hand gripped his back as her nails dug into his skin and my soul simultaneously. His pant increased along with his moans from the rotation of her grind that I knew vividly.

"How long…?" My voice cracked. "How long have you been fucking him?" I intruded as they begin their climax unable to stop their powerful orgasms without warning. She opened her eyes in shock, looked at me with an expression of regret, deepened the grasp she had on him to prevent herself from falling as he jerked inside of her and whaled upon his uncontrollable release, and let the tears fall from her eyes the way her cream rolled down her walls betraying me and mixing with his seeds now running wild inside her valley.

"Cameron!" Loveless called out to me.

"How long?" I questioned as dude pulled up his pants and grabbed his shirt off the floor. I stepped to the side as he stopped momentarily at my side and said, "Sorry shit went down like this Shorty!", and then made his way to and through the front door. It was not until then with the smell of her scent, her honey dip on him, that my mind connected with my heart and I became heartbroken and enraged at the same time and I could not shelter my tears any longer. She came over to wipe away my tears and said," I'm so sorry!"

I jerked away before her finger touched my skin. I snapped, "Don't you dare touch me with his smell on you…Oh GOD, he's in you right now! You fucked him… and you fucked him raw!" The thought made me nauseous and the fact that I had been licking her made me run to the bathroom and vomit.

"It was a mistake."

"You damn right it was a mistake!" I yelled as I began to yank my clothes off the hangers from my side of the walk-in closet.

"Cameron, what are you doing?"

"What does it look like, I'm leaving! What I should have done a long time ago… The first time you put your hands on me… I should have left then, but no I stayed… I stayed even after you broke your promise to me and did it again I stayed. I stayed and endured sleepless nights, because we fought all night long, to cover bruises. Every time you felt insecure and said that I was fooling around because I was too tired to make love to you!"

"Let's talk this out." she said as she walked closer to me.

"Ok let's talk this out!" I slung another empty luggage bag on the bed and looked her in the eyes and questioned,

"How many times did you fuck him?"

"Cameron."

"How many, two, four, six, wait the whole time we have been together Loveless?" My stomach knotted up from her eyes answer.

"Baby I love you."

"How dare you say that to me? How dare you? Love me… the audacity! I'll tell you what love is! Hell, I showed you what love is. I got shunned from my church for you… Disowned by my family for you… I even backed away from the relationship with my best friend so that I could stroke your ego at will! She tried to tell me but I refused to listen. You were a jealous and abusive woman but I never thought that you would betray me. I would have bet my life on that, that you loved me too much to do that!"

"And I do love you…Baby… Please I made mistakes plenty, but I don't want to lose you!" She grabbed my hands to stop me from tossing my things into the over filled bag.

"NO CONDOMS! I guess I did bet my life on you…you better hope for both our sakes that all the tests I take first thing in the morning say negative!" I said as I pulled my hands away from her.

"Marshall… Dianah Marshall…" The nurse dressed in white scrubs with stethoscopes all over the top calls out over the crowded room, never taking her eyes off of the manila folder in her hand.

Dianah stands up and walks toward her and her unknown fate alone as we did the only thing we could do in this situation, wait and pray.

"Thank you Buddha." Raven touch my face with her hand and caresses my heart with her eyes.

"Betrayal hurts, even when it's assistant is your own denial!" I say and shake off the memory of my past actions, grateful I' m no longer a victim of the sad reality of when the cycle that I broke goes unbroken.

"I can't believe that Vance has been playing Russian roulette with her life for years!" I watch the emotion sway in Ravens face.

"I despise that he was forced to live his life this way causing him and Dianah to become another statistic." I reply honestly.

"That he had to live his life this way…umm, and which way would that be? As a lying, manipulative coward that not only devalued his own life by having unprotected sex, but the life of the woman that shares his bed and that he's supposed to love, and who happens to be one of my best friends that is now in-between a wing and a prayer for a healthy life that will not be cut short do to his carelessness!" She finally takes a breath and looks at me with the lines defined across her forehead that yells, I can't believe you just said that…

"As a black man that is pressured to fill the distorted requirements of the black community to qualify his status as a man, when they don't even know the meaning themselves. Man! Deceitfully defined from the ghettos to the church houses… While brothers on the block press each other to show and prove their ability to be hood, passing along the neighborhood hood rats like a rite of passage and leaving behind hollow minds, bodies, and souls of their black sisters… not to mention the off springs that could belong to any one of them yet claimed by none, because their mother was the hoe! To the church boys that learn early on that Sunday school is the place to pick up 'the good girls', middle and upper class girls that are not only down with sexing but sexing raw because they stay on birth control. You were in as long as you followed the cardinal rule… hook ups stay among the members of the church and didn't get back to the community or their parents, courtesy of living your life as a Christian. Let's face it Boobie, the only thing worse than being a gay black man in our community is being a working black man, not living off of his mother or sister, and dating a white woman!" I shake my head sadden by what we have become in this day and age.

"I see your point but I'm sorry… there is no excuse for Vance to have not used a fucking condom or at the very least let her choose whether or not to deal with him knowing him in his entirety, the way she was honest with him!"

"Honest with him? She wasn't honest with herself… that's why she didn't see what was in front of her!"

"What do you mean?" Raven says protectively.

"She was lying to him as well as herself. She was so afraid of being a lesbian that she didn't see him for who he was, only as who she needed him to be, her normalcy!" Raven sat back in the hard chair, pressed the palms of her hands on her throbbing temples, closed her eyes and sat speechless for a moment, as did I.

Chase James

I scoot the chair inches away from my dining room table and close my eyes. I press my knuckles against my forehead hoping the images in my mind would go as blank as the white envelope containing the results of the paternity test that I placed on it about an hour ago but they don't. And the visions of Zachary Steele Jr. flood my mind. I see his muscles flex with each curl of his arms before he finishes his last set of his workout. I see him tilt his head back and let the sweat run through his low fuzz cut and down his muscular neck. I see his pale pink lips as he presses them against the rim of the 24oz water bottle and I can't stop myself from envisioning him pressing them against Kioni's skin. I grit my teeth to keep my emotions in check because I feel rage building inside me now the same way it did when I was less than ten feet away from him, fighting the urge to unload my glock into him as he rubs the towel over his head and face, wiping away the pouring sweat. I watch his movement as he walks towards the showers along with several other women that find his looks appealing. I walk over and put the towel inside a plastic bag the same way I placed the Wine glasses and silverware with Zachary Steele Sr.'s DNA on them the night before. I open my eyes and tight my hands into fists. I hate that I can't fool my own mind and deny that I saw Deshaun's features all over Zachary's face.

"Hey baby. I didn't know you were already home. I would have picked something up for dinner on my way in." Kioni says as she walks over and plants a soft kiss on my lips. She pulls away slowly and looks at me, because my lips didn't greet hers with their usual intensity.

"Come here." I say as I take her hand and guide her onto my lap.
"Chase, what's wrong? Your look is scaring me." She places one of her hands against my left cheek and the other on my arm.

"I'm sorry. I don't mean to scare you." I look into Kioni's eyes and know that I have failed her so many times in the past, with broken promises. So I can't blame her for thinking I'm gonna do it again.

"Baby what's going on?" Her eyes search mine for understanding. I place my fingers onto her chin and kiss her with all the tenderness her love has instilled in me. I kiss her long and deep before I answer her with words.

"The results came in today." I let my eyes lead hers to the envelope on the table.

"Which one…" her words are low.

"I didn't look."

"Why didn't you look at the results?" I feel her body tense up, so I take her hands into mine and say…

"Either we do this together, or we don't do this at all." She finally allows herself to turn around and I see that her eyes are filled with water.

"Ok baby." She wipes away the tears that stream her cheeks and smiles at me, and I smile back.

She pulls a chair next to me and picks up the envelope. Kioni looks at me, takes a deep breath, then she removes the papers from the envelope and unfolds them. I watch her eyes scan the words on the paper and focus in on the results. Tears flood her face and she begins to rock back and forth. I want to give her the space she needs but we both know that she has had to face this thing alone for far too long. I take her in my arms and wrap her in the warmth of my love. She holds on to me tightly as I kiss her cheek over and again, reassuring her of my love. Kioni loosens her embrace without saying a word and shows me the results. The words seem magnified. 99.9999% Zachary Steele Sr. is the biological father of Deshaun Andre Wils. I feel Kioni's eyes watching me, waiting for my reaction.

"This is only one piece to a puzzle." I say as I fold the papers back up, place them back into the envelope and push it into my back pocket.

"Baby, I'm sorry!" Kioni wraps her arms around my neck and I feel her heart beating through her chest.

"You have no reason to be. You and Deshaun are my blessings!" I pick her up and carry her to the master bathroom and run her a bath.

I take my time and wash every part of her body before I take her to bed and cover with my love.

Now that I'm finish tying up all the loose ends needed to ensure Kioni will never have to live her life in fear that either of the Steeles' will ever reenter her life and destroy what she has worked so hard to create for herself and Deshaun. It's time for me to take the last step in my master plan.

"What do you have on your plate for the day?" I ask Sims as I step closer to him at his desk.

"Nothing that can't be handled tomorrow, what you need?" He lays down the paper he was reading before I interrupted him.

"I can use some back up." My tone tells him it's serious.

"Does this have anything to do with that info we came across earlier in the week?" Sims question is referring to the Steele's records, financial details, shady backgrounds, and hidden secrecies that he help me uncover.

"Everything to..."

"Where are we headed?" Sims stands up and grabs his blazer off the back of his chair, before I can fully answer him.

"Steele Incorporated."

"Good afternoon, How my I help you?"

"I'm here to see the Steele's." I say as though they are expecting me.

"I'm sorry but they are both in a meeting right now…" Sims and I both notice the secretary eyes glance at the double doors at the center of the hallway so we head for them.

"You can't go in there!" she tries to catch up to me before I reach them but Sims shows her his badge and ushers her back to her desk.

I turn the knobs and push the doors open with force, startling everyone in the room.

"Who the hell are you?" Zachary Sr.'s voice vibrates from the head of the conference table at me like I'm one of his insubordinates.

The arrogance in his voice ignites my rage. "I'm impending karma, snake-motherfucker!" I say as I walk up to him and toss the thick manila folder in front of him.

"Clear the room!" Zachary Jr. orders as he stands from his set at the left of his father and the mix of black and blue suits scatter out of the room with haste.

"I guess the appropriate question to ask you, is whether or not you know who I am?" Zachary Sr. says through words laced with laughter.

"I think that you should open it." Zachary Jr. pushes the folder to his father.
Zachary Sr. opens it with frustration and within seconds the smug drains from his face and it goes pale as he is hit with the news that he is not only a rapist but he is a father again.

"What is it exactly that she wants?" His words are full of distain.

"What she wants, is to erase very time you fucking held her down and raped her or forced your teenage son to do the same! What she wants is to get back the innocence that you took from her every time you covered her mouth and muffled her screams. But since your money can't buy that the way it bought her mother's silence. You're going to do the next best thing. You are going to deposit the amounts listed into the accounts that have already been set up for you, then you are going to stay the hell away from her and her son indefinitely. As for the stock Jr., here will be the go between with her liaison." My words are sharp and cause Zachary Jr.'s face to fill with shame as he drops into his set speechless.

"What makes you think that I will give Kioni any part of my company?" Zachary Sr. says enraged at the terms of the legal documents in his hands.

The sound of her name coming out of his mouth sets me a blazes and I slam my badge down on the table and say "Because what people do to gain power is only a mere fraction of what they will do to keep it!"

Zachary Sr. looks at my badge and back at me, and then he picks up a pen.

"I know all about you looking out for them through the years. I have every confidence that you have their best interest at heart but from this moment on make sure you remain in the dark completely!" Zachary Jr. looks at me and I can see that his eyes are full of painful regret.

I take my time looking over the signed copies before putting them neatly into the folder. I stand up and adjust my clothes. I leave their copies on the table and place my badge back on my waste.

"If either one of you go anywhere near Kioni or Deshaun, I will bring this building and your world crashing down around you!" I say with my back to them then I exit the doors I entered!

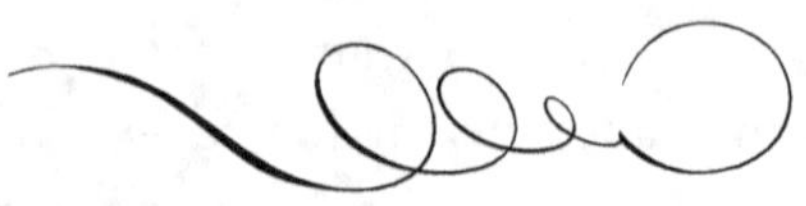

Remy Gamble

I look in the small mirror on the back of the sun visor in my car. I suck my teeth and touch my face lightly around my stinging open flesh. I grit my teeth and wipe the running mixture of blood and beer from my eye with my shirt sleeve. The whole right side of my face is throbbing so I don't know how much longer I have before my eye swells shut on me. One thing is for sure there is no way that I can let my old girl see me like this. I crank up my ride and peel out of Kioni's drive way. I get halfway up the block and see Jodie braking on his cell phone. I can't believe that he swung on me like I was the one his dude was fucking. I drive pass him and leave his ass in my rearview.

"Baby girl I call out for the third time and bang on the door again. I know that it doesn't take a lot for the sound to fill the room.

"What the fuck is your problem making all this noise in the hallway?" Ebonee yells as she flings the room door open.

"It's a hotel… I didn't know you were in the shower lil mama. As you can see a nigga fucked up right now." I look at her wrapped in a towel and water dripping from her wet hair.

"Omg what the fuck happened to you?" Ebonee's tone softens when she sees my face. Ebonee's eye scans the rest of my body as she steps to the side and lets me in. She closes and locks the door behind me.

"Everybody be on that tell the truth shit until it's time for them to do the same." I say as I sit down in the chair by the table and feel a sharp pain on my left side that makes me cringe.

"What are you talking about Remy?" Ebonee asks me as she comes out of the bathroom with a wet towel in her hand and she begins to dab clean around my wound.

"Ms. Do Right finally got some damn act right. That's what I'm talking about." I say through laughter that causes me more pain but remembering the look on Dianah's face when she realized who Jodye was makes the pain I'm feeling worth it.

"What did you do?" Ebonee stepped back holding the white towel with my blood stain on it in her hand and cut her eyes at me.

"It was price watching them befriend each other for over an hour never knowing that they have both been fucking the same guy at the same time for years. But when Jodie pulled out the picture he kept in his wallet of him and Heavenly chocolate I thought I would die." I'm laughing so hard that it takes me a min to realize that Ebonee isn't laughing with me.

"Heavenly chocolate?" she asks moving her hand from in front of her mouth.

"Oh my bad, Heavenly chocolate, is the nick name Jodie calls Vance; the dude that was in the picture with Dianah I showed you in her guess room." I refresh her memory.

"If you knew that why would you take him with you? Wait you planned for them to find out about each other." Ebonee crosses her arms in front of her chest and gives me a 'that's so fuck up' look.

"Damn skippy I did! It was far time for her ass to see what it feels like to have her shit broadcasted." I feel completely justified in what I did.

"Wow and I bet you don't see anything wrong in what you did!"

"Hell, naw I did her a favor. You never know how many other men he is sleeping with then running back to her. That shit is unhealthy." I rub my chin and think about what I just said for a minute.

"I can't believe you really believe the shit you say!" Ebonee shakes her head at me and causes my energy to change.

"Let me guess you want to jump on that friendship bullshit, right? Well, where was that friendship when Dianah cost me my best friend, huh? Did you forget she's the one who caused all this shit to go down when all she had to do was keep her fuckin mouth shut?" I look around the room and stop at the boxes with all Ebonee's things in them point them out to her.

"Remy, it's always about what somebody did or didn't do for you. You never once claim your own shit, never. Dianah didn't make you lose your friendship with Ivory you did that all by yourself when chose to pursue your best friends girl. Dianah was a friend to me that is all she ever was to me. I betrayed her friendship by fucking you in her fucking house! And as for the boxes you so eagerly pointed out, that's all you."

"How the fuck is this on me? You on some bullshit now!" I say with a mean mug on my face.

"Yeah, your right I was on the bullshit you feed to me. Every time you would tell me how you would be there for me whenever I needed you. How you wanted to show me what love is supposed to feel like. You know what for the first time Remy; I'm seeing you for who you really are. You are a parasite that clings onto and sucks the blood from anyone that is kind enough to offer you warmth until it's withered, and then you move onto the next unexpecting host."

"What the fuck did you just say to me?" I feel heat from her words flood my body and I raise from the chair ready for battle.

"You heard exactly what I said. I didn't stutter." Ebonee looks at me with discuss on her face.

"I'm a parasite huh, baby girl? All I tried to do is right by you. When Ivory was treating your ass like an unwanted house nigga, I was the one putting a smile on your face and dick in your ass." I say with a large smirk on my face

"You gotta go." Ebonee says and opens the room door.

"All bullshit aside though if you had stood up for yourself with Ivory like this you would still be the one sharing her bed instead of the stripper that she so quickly replaced you with." I shake my head at Ebonee and walk through the door and stop in the hall way.

I don't turn around when she slams the door. I scroll through my contacts touch the name Diamond and hit the send button. "Hey baby, some shit went down tonight and I need you to hold your nigga down for a couple of days. You got me. Bet that up. Oh yeah have a Xanax and a stiff drink waiting for me I have a headache out of this world!"

Dianah Marshall

The cold raindrops pierce through the fabric of my clothes and cover my heated flesh, as I rush out of my vehicle. I walk towards the wooden French doors and ring the doorbell. I don't know why I'm here, maybe it's because some part of me blames her for my dealings with Vance. The whole ordeal of having to be tested because Vance was sleeping with a man while proclaiming to love me… had me more terrified then I have ever been in my life… even after receiving the results of a clean bill of health from all my STD testing earlier today, I've been overwhelmed with emotions. I think about how Vance's dishonesty placed me at so many risks… I think about how I focused on loving him because I was told it was the right thing to do. Yet my heart leads me here, back to the same place it led me so many years ago when I realized I was attracted to woman.

"Dianah, what's wrong?" my mother asks me as she looks me up and down, honing in on the tears that somehow stood out from the wetness that drenched me from my head to before she took my hand and pulls me into shelter from the rain.

"Get out of those wet clothes before you get sick," my mother orders, then turns and hurries up the stairs. I could hear doors opening as and closing seconds behind each other as I shed my clothes. Then I see my mother return with a plush towel in one hand and one of her silk Kimonos in the other.

"Dry yourself off and put this on, I'll put your things in the dryer, let's go into the kitchen and get something hot in you before you catch pneumonia." My mother takes them and begins to head to the washroom when I touch her arm and ask,

"Where is daddy?"

"Tokyo, business conference," she says and continues her stride.

I slide my skin into my mother's silk robe as though it belongs to me. I tie the strap, then wrap the now damp towel around my hair and tuck the loose end under the side. I walk into the kitchen just as the tea kettle begins to whistle. My mother looks back at me, searches my eyes for a moment, then she pours the boiling water into the coffee mugs. She adds honey and cream to them as though it is not late night for some and early morning for others, then she walks over to the table where I sit awaiting her. I look at my mother. Admire the elegance that she possesses; admire the skin tone that she has passed down to me. I inhale her essence that's always been sent through the same sweet aroma since I was a little girl. I remember many times being with her and people stop in their tracks to take a longer glance at her beauty, men and women alike. I wonder now if she is truly happy with all that she has attained in her lifetime.

"Ok, I'm ready to listen to whatever it is that has you this upset." She says as she takes a sip of her chamomile tea.

"And once again I am a child, nervous like the first and only time I ever broke curfew and my mother knows it. So she puts down her mug and places her soft hand on mine.

"You are shaking. Talk to me!" my mother says as she moves her chair closer to me.

"Mama, I love you." I swallow hard. "I believed everything you told me about living my life this way, but you were so wrong mama." My words brought back the tears.

"Wrong about what?" my mother squints her eyes and tilts her head a bit at my statement, but does not let the temper she has risen yet.

"You told me that loving a woman was wrong, hell impossible…"

"Dianah, we settled this years ago." My mother removes her hand from mine and takes a hard sip of her tea and shakes her head slowly. I can tell that she is about to lose her reserve by the flare in her nostrils and the arch in her brow that she also passed down to me.

"No mama, you told me what I was going to do with my feelings and how I was to deal with women. You made it clear what you would accept from me and I loved and needed you. I wanted your acceptance because I couldn't bear living without your love, so I did as I was told." I look at my mother as she looks at me and I try to wipe away my tears.

"And my expectations for you are still the same. You are my daughter. You have a successful career, you're educated, beautiful, and you have a man that most women would die for. And whom might I add adores you. So these feelings that you are battling with will dissipate baby, they always do." My mother places her hand on my cheek and wipes away my tears with her thumbs and smiles at me gently.

"Vance..." saying his name sends my heat barreling through my chest.

"Vance doesn't adore me. He never has, mother!" I say with bitterness.

"You're talking crazy. Throughout the years of my interaction with him, he has shown nothing but adoration for you."

"I used to think so too, but... but now I know that what you saw was a liar covering his tracks!" I stand up and turn away from my mother.

"Ok Dianah, what the hell is going on? Did Vance put his hands on you?" My mother questions me as she grips my chin with her fingers and looks me over to see if she has missed a bruise on me somewhere.

"He didn't hit me, but honestly I would've preferred that he had to the pain that I'm feeling in my heart. I feel so betrayed, betrayed by him, betrayed by society's rules, and in a way I feel betrayed by you as well." I look at my mother. I see the look of concern blend with confusion.

"Betrayed by me? How might I ask did I betrayed you Dianah?" my mother asks as she stands face to face with me.

"Because you told me that life with a man would be a secure one. That it was the natural thing in life where love formulates, where love resonates, that not only the world but God smiles on the union."

"And you feel betrayed by me how Dianah?" My mother is clearly agitated now.

"Because you told me to sacrifice being who I am, to compromise my existence from what came natural to me. And in doing so, my being with Vance, has been nothing but a lie. Even down to the image of him being my man, my safety, the love of my life, my understanding friend, Vance never loved me, like I never fully desired him. Even when the very thing that kept me running back to him was his so called understanding and unconditional love. When I told him about my dealings with women, I thought he was the most compassionate and confident man in the world, but he is a coward. He hid behind that smile of his and I should've seen it years ago." I feel the anger inside of me swell and collide with the hurt I feel. Things between Vance and I are over and I don't regret leaving him before I found out that he had been deceiving me all these years. I have to admit that the fact that I was always honest with him cuts like a knife. Memories and emotions run wild and my soul gives way to the rampage and I fall into my mother's arms. I feel her hold me tight and give way to her anger. I hold on to her, feel her concern for me, and in that moment I reveal what was kept from me for years.

"Vance has been sleeping with a man the whole time we've been together. And I never knew mama, I never knew!" I feel her body tense all over. Hear the air brush against my ear as she takes in a deep breath.

"Are you sure? There must be some kind of mistake." She asks without letting me go.

"There's no mistake mother. I have seen his lover with my own two eyes."

"What do you mean you seen his lover?" My mother looks at me with disbelief written all over her face and enveloping her body language.

"I met him at a get together a couple of friends of mine were having. Neither of us knew that we were sleeping with the same man until he showed a picture of his lover that he has had for over fifteen years that finally wanted to call it off to save the relationship with the so called woman he loves. When I looked at the picture of the two of them together, I couldn't believe my eyes. I shake my head, slowly from side to side.

"Fifteen years… Oh my!" my mother held her hand over her chest, then walked over and picked up a bottle of Moet and two glasses and brought them over to the table and filled them to the brim.

Dianah Marshall

I reach into my bag to retrieve my cell phone so that I can call Raven and let her know that I'm on I-95 heading home like I told her I would when I texted her last night explaining that I was not in an emotional state to talk to anyone let alone deal with Vance, so I went to the one place I knew he wouldn't dare show his face. As soon as I touch it, it vibrates in my hand from all the alerts on my main screen… sixty-nine missed calls, and two hundred unread text messages all from Vance. I grit my teeth and try to balance the pounding of my head and the burning ache in my chest. I ignore them all and scroll my contact list till I reach Raven's number and press the send button.

"Are you ok? Are you still at your parents?" Raven questions me before I have the chance to say hello. I could hear the love and concern in her voice that comes from years of friendship.

"I have a migraine that just won't let up. I'm on 95." I rub my fingers over the center of my forehead and allow my eyes to close briefly.

"Did you… tell them why you…" her tone's nervous for me.

"She knows… It was just the two of us… dad was away on business…" my words are heavy.

"How did that… what did she say when you told her about Vance's secret life?" I could hear the worry build in her voice because she knows all too well the nature of my relationship with my mother.

"She was in shock and disbelief at first. Then she tried to make me see reason… She told me that it was clear that he loves me, despite his lapse in judgment… She told me that he had to have seen the errors of his ways to have put an end to… in her words "whatever he was doing!"… Oh yeah and need I forget that he has allowed me to have my little flings over the years."

"Di…" Raven sigh is full of compassion.

"It's ok… By the time we finished drinking the third bottle of wine the gloves came off and we both said some things that were hurtful and comforting… until we gave in to exhaustion." I feel emotion billing inside me with each thought of my mother's beliefs.

"I hate to tell you this right now, but Vance came by here last night looking for you… and Kioni swears she saw Vance outside her place early this morning when she was leaving for work!"

"You're kidding me! I… I… never meant to get you guys mixed in my drama!" I can feel the stress filling my head like liquid and shifting as a turn off the Interstate on my exit.

"Dianah don't be silly; you are not the one that created this chaos… and I'm sure that Kioni feels the same!" I can hear a change in her breathing.

"What are you doing?"

"I'm tying my sneakers. So, I can be on my way to you. Why?" her voice tells me that her coming over is not up for debate, so I don't.

"Because you sound winded!" I reply without resistance.

"Hell I'm getting old dammit!" We both laugh hard for a moment.

"I'll see you in a few." Her words are laced with kisses.

"Ok… see you when you get here." Mines are laced with gratitude, we hang up.

I see Vance's Escalade parked in front of my front door on the curved part of my drive way before I make my way to it. Just before I turn into the part of my driveway that leads to my garage, I see Vance pacing back and forth in front of it. So, I don't press the clicker that's clamped to my sun visor that will raise the garage door and grant me access to my home because it would do the same for him. My every intent in this moment is on pulling in front of the garage, placing the gear into park, and taking the keys out of the ignition. But the second his eyes make contact with mine all logic is lost. I grip the steering wheel and press the gas pedal to the floorboard. I hear the thud of Vance's body hitting the hood of my car as he leaps onto it like a frog leaping from one lily pad to his next to avoid being molded over.

"Dianah stop the car! Please stop the got damn car and let me explain…" Vance pleads in a frantic voice as he tries to hold on for survival.

"Explain what? Explain how you were holding hands, standing close, smiling with him?" I think of him all booed up in that fucking picture and slam my foot on the brake. Gravity takes over and the weight that he has been carrying sends him to the pavement. I throw the car in reverse and gain enough distance to see him trying to stand up and my jealously forces the gear stick into drive, my rage supplies the gas, while my pain steers toward the cause of all three for the second time.

Vance dives out of the way of my car and into the shrubs that line my driveway within inches of me hitting him and seconds before I run into the garage door.

I slam the gear stick into park, jump out my car slamming the door without thought as I make my way to the bushes that shelter Vance.

"How long have you known dude?" I yell allowing my words to reach him before I do.

"I know you are angry, but you could have killed me!" Vance says in a shaky voice as he dusts the dirt and debris off his black t shirt and denim jeans.

"I saw the fucking picture of the two of you!" I say as I smack him across the left side of his face with my right hand.

"I'm sorry that I hurt you, can't we get back what we had?" He pulls me close to him, his voice fills my head and I feel the warmth of his chocolate skin next to mine. I inhale his familiar scent and in this moment we are lovers again.

"Don't, Vance I can't get the thought of the two of you out of my head." I shake my head no and push him away from me.

"I wish that I could take it all back!" His eyes fill with water.

"How fucking long have you known him, Vance?"

"Since high school..." His words knock the wind out of me and I struggle to breathe.

"I never meant to hurt you... I can fix this... I'm sorry... I'm so sorry, I love you Dianah... please let me fix this!" he reaches out to touch me and I push his hands away.

"Don't you dare say that to me! Sorry? You're not sorry! You're only sorry you got caught! Sorry that I know the truth about you now! You're sorry I know who you really are! Sorry... The hell with sorry, I know who you never were, who you never will be... I was your fool all along huh? I tilt my head to look him in his lying eyes and tears of anger and betrayal flood my face. The thought of him with another man makes me sick to my stomach.

"I need you to forgive me. Please forgive me. I love you!" he stands with his arms out stretched.

"Love me, if you loved me you would have never lied to me... You let me be in this without you or my consent...Hell, you...you were never fucking mine!" I replay that fact that Jody was with him before we even meet in my mind. I charge him letting my hurt and betrayal crash into his skin as I slap him across his face a few more times before he gets a grip of my wrist.

"I never would have had a chance!" His words take my breath away then cause me to become livid, so I let my words do to him what he is preventing me to express physically.

"How dare I not want to taste you when I enjoy eating pussy… Then I couldn't love you! All the while, you craved a taste for dick yourself… So you forced it on me as though I was supposed to have the same love, which I didn't, I never have! I just wanted to please you… Be a good woman to and for you… I wanted to love you as strong as you loved me… Or at least as much as you said you loved me… and I thought you loved me for who I was, when all the while, you loved the cover that fucking me provided you!" I watch the life drain from his face with cold eyes as my words pierce is heart and he lets go of my wrist.

"I do love you and my love has never failed you… I never raised my hand to you or treated you with disrespect, the way my father treated my mother… I never left you lonely…There has never been a time when you needed for anything that I didn't provide… And whenever you felt unsure I was there to hold your hand through it… I've always had your back… I wish that I could change my past mistakes… I wish you could see the love that I have for you." His words are soft like each one comes with a sharp pain attached.

"I wish I could close my eyes and pretend that I didn't get my heart ripped out of my chest when I saw that picture of you… pretend that everything that I ever known about you was still true… Pretend that you don't disgust me right now… and this disgust I feel for you has nothing to do with you fucking another man… and everything to do with you putting my fucking health at risk because you are self-serving and dishonest… I wish that I could pre, Pretend that his name wasn't the one you called out while you were fucking me!" I feel my emotions run down my face and it's as warm as the blood boiling in my veins as I wipe them away with the back of my hand. I walk back to my car and yank the keys out of the ignition and head for my front door.

"Dianah, please forgive me, I was wrong but I'll make things rights if you give me the chance. I need you!" Vance grabs me by my waste, falls to his knees, presses his head into my stomach, and begs for my forgiveness.

"You had plenty of time to right this wrong Vance. I don't know if I will ever forgive you maybe with time the pain loving you has cost me will heal and forgiveness will surface. I told you months ago that we were over and I meant it. So when you leave here please make it the last time you come by to my house, don't call my phone, don't call my job, and don't you ever fucking show up at my friend's house looking for me again. I have moved on with my life so please do the same." I maneuver my body away from him and take a few steps before he grabs my right wrist.

"How you just gonna walk away from me like there was no love between us, when you said that you would always have love for me?" his voice was as strong as his grip. So I couldn't be happier to see Raven coming up to us.

"Let her go Vance!" Raven yells in a protective tone when she seen me struggling to get lose and begins to pry away his hold on me one finger at a time.

"I'm just trying to talk to her!" Vance cuts his eyes at raven then stairs at me.

"There is nothing left to talk about." I hold up the palms of my hands.

"Vance I think you should go!" Raven says as she places her body in between the both of us. Emotions are at a dangerous high and we all know it.

Kioni Wils

"I'm so glad that you don't mind having lunch here." I say as I kiss Dianah on her cheek and walk over and sit my bag down on the chair in the living room.

"Child please. You know I would rather kick my shoes off, unbutton the top button on my pants, and put in work in the comfort of home any day." Raven says as she greets me with a kiss of her own.

"You know that's right. Besides you sounded like you could use some QT time with your girls anyway." Dianah says while she hands me a glass of Moscato.

I take a few sips and sit it down on the floor stand beside the floor cushions she has set up.

"Hope you are okay with sushi and yes I did order you a double order of shrimp tempura." Raven says beating me to the punch of asking.

"It's perfect! I don't think I would be able to hold down anything heavy right now." I sit on the cushion and fold my legs until they are comfortably positioned Indian style.

"So you ready to get whatever is on your mind off your chest?" Raven asks then takes a bite of her crab rangoon.

"I have so much to say. I don't really know where to start." I look at them and see their love patiently waiting for me.

"Start anywhere. Once it's out we can make sense of things." Dianah says.

"I got the paternity test back and although it was hard to see physical proof that such a horrific act happened to me, in a way it's a relief. Because know I know which one of them fathered my son." I feel my emotions begin to stir. So I shift my body a little before I continue. "My mother's face went pale in that hospital room all those years ago because she saw in my Deshaun's face what the results confirmed, that her husband fathered her 16 year old daughter's child." I feel the warmth of tears trail my face.

"Kioni, are you okay?" Dianah asks with a look as though she wants to come hold me but she doesn't move.

"I am now. But when I first read the words, it was a little too much for me to bear. I couldn't stop having flashbacks of those moments. And when I showed the results to Chase, I wasn't sure of what her reaction would be." I wipe away my tears and feel the warmth of her love inside me.

"And what was her reaction?" Raven asks with a look on her face that tells me that she would resort to bodily harm if Chase had been anything less than supportive and Dianah's say she would assist her.

"Chase was amazing! She took the papers out of my hand and told me there where a piece to a much bigger puzzle that at the time I had no idea about. Then she told and showed me how much she loved me." I look at them and smile and they smile back through tears of their own.

"That's what I'm saying." Dianah says with her hand up against the center of her chest.

"It's crazy how long I feared her knowing what I had been through, feared that she would walk away from me. That she would never be able to see me through all my tainted stains. It's surreal that she has done the complete opposite." I am over whelmed by the love of my life.

"That's love." Raven says and exhales slowly.

"Okay, there's more." I say as they quickly give me their attention after we all take a few more sips of our drinks.

"So a few days ago, Chase hands me a large manila folder and tells me that because I trusted her enough to share my fears with her even after all the pain she has caused me, she took the liberty of having them permanently removed from my life."

"Let me find out that Chase has some game!" Dianah says playfully and Raven cuts her a look and says don't pay her any mind, go on.

"When I opened the envelope, I almost passed out. I couldn't believe my eyes. There were legal documents for trust funds for me and Deshaun and stock for the Steele's company, all signed by Zachary Steele Sr. himself." Even though I say the words I can hardly believe it's real.

"Are you serious?" Dianah questions to make sure she heard me correctly.

"How did Chase make that happen?" Raven asks as she sits up at attention.

"I asked her the same thing. Chase said that she had done a lot of digging into the Steele's background when I told about the molestation and uncovered things that would put him away for a long time and destroy the empire he built if they were ever exposed." I shrug my shoulders.

"Humph." Dianah turns up her lips.

"I bet. Slimy bastards." Raven rolls her eyes.

"Long story short, she burst into their meeting and faced my damn demons for me. And not only can I retire right now if I choose to, but they can never contact or come near Deshaun or me again. Or as Chase put it, she would bring their world and their company crashing down around them.

"Oh my God, Kioni. I'm so glad that you can finally live your life without looking over your shoulders," Dianah says as she walks over to me on her knees and hugs and kisses me.

"So am I. I told you things have a way of working themselves out, even when we think there is no foreseeable resolve." Raven says as she does the same.

We wipe our faces and laugh at how emotional we all become for, with, and about each other.

"Okay, okay, okay, enough about me. How are things with you guys?" I ask and pick up my tempura.

"Honestly, things couldn't be better. I didn't think that I could fall any deeper for Ramona, but I have to admit something. You guys were right about when you said that letting a woman use a strap on me would be way different from all the times I have strapped them. Being strapped takes things to a whole other level!" Dianah says catching us off guard causing Raven to damn near spit her wine across the room.

We all laugh because we know that it's true then we acknowledge the step that Dianah has just admitted she has taken.

"So when am I gonna get to meet the notorious woman that stole my best friend's heart?" Raven asks lovingly.

"Yes, I'm dying to meet her too." I join Raven.

"The same time I get to meet Ms. N'dia!" Dianah says with a smile and leans into Raven's arm.

"I think that would be great, because I think the both of you have kept your women to yourselves long enough!" I say with a playful pout.

We were all smiles with love being the cause.

Chase James

"Chase, when your last session with me came to an end, you said love is more. I would like for you to pick up from there." Dr. Nina Myles says as she places her notebook on her lap and touches her bottom lip with the tip of her pen.

I look at the rain tap against the window from the chaise placed a few feet away from the chair she is sitting in.

"I think that love is more than all the hurt and pain it caused me or the simplistic tones used whenever someone told me they loved me. And more than my own use of it in turn."

"And what hurt and pain is that?"

"The numerous broken bones, black eyes, and swollen flesh that I suffered through because he didn't want me." I look at Nina Myles, unafraid of letting her see my truth.

"Who didn't want you?"

"My daddy. He never wanted me, but I longed to be adored by him." I feel the tears fill up and pour out of my eyes.

Dr. Nina Myles doesn't say anything. I've come to understand that's just her unspoken way of telling me to take the time I need, then proceed.

"My daddy already didn't want me. So when he realized that I was into girls early on, he despised me. So I guess he felt that he could beat it out of me."

I look at the rain and think about how people say they hate the rain all time, but without it everything would wither away.

"Chase."

"Yes."

"What did your mother say about your father's methods for dealing with your sexuality?" Nina Myles says bringing back to my emotions.

"She told me, she told me that she loved me!" My own words take my breath away because I realized for the first time that Kioni would say the same thing to me after I was the cause of her pain.

"How did that make you feel?"

"It made me feel like it was me. Like I was the cause of his rage. Like I wasn't worth enough to be loved. Because when he would kick me like I was a dog that bit him, she did nothing to stop him but told me that she was sorry and that she loved me after the beating was over."

"Do you think she loved you?"

"In her own way. I think she just got caught up in the way she thought things should be." I see the beauty of my mother's face as I close my eyes for a minute and let my tears wash that image away.

"I mean before Kioni, I never knew what it was like for someone to hold me through the night." I smile at the thought of the most beautiful person in my life.

"Your mother never held you?" She asks and writes a few notes.

"Once. I was twelve. It was the first time he broke something on me and I was in so much pain that I cried for hours on end. She came in my room and got in my bed with me. She took me into her arms and held me close until I fell asleep, but when I woke up she was gone."

"Did you ever tell Kioni that?"

"No. I never told anyone, these things are the secrets that my mother and I share." I feel my body trembling on the inside.

"After all the recent events the two of you shared, do you plan on sharing the secrets you are keeping with her?"

"Yes, but the time is not right yet."

"And why isn't it the right time?"

"Because I haven't earned her forgiveness yet."

"You don't think that she has forgiven you even after what you have done for her and Deshaun?"

"Kioni has forgiven me because she loves me. I want her trust back. And I plan on earning it by loving her immensely. And when I'm sure that I have it, I will tell her all the awful things that once made me the person I used to be, before she helped me understand that love in its purest form is not one action but a multitude of emotions stimulated into positive actions that work together to secure, empower, uplift, inspire, encourage, and illuminate the beauty of one's soul." I look at Dr. Nina Myles. She has her elbows on the arms of the sofa chair, her fingers are interlocked within each other, and her chin is slightly touching them. She inhales then lets out a calm exhale that transcends a smile, just before the buzzer sounds alerting us that the session is over.

Ebonee Price

Someone once told me that life never leaves a woman's body without the woman recognizing and mourning the separation from her in some way. From cramping, when she is passing life through her menstruation, the pain of her body stretching and tearing her during birth, the physical and emotional pain of a miscarriage, and there is even a never ending pain that a woman goes through when she has an abortion, whether it's by choice, force, or circumstance. But as I sit in sleepless solitude, I can't help but wonder if a woman ever feels pain when the life that leaves her body is very own. I get up from the chair and walk into the bathroom. I look in the mirror and I feel like an old baby doll that has been replaced by the latest Barbie society has put on the shelf. But I can't help but remember the time that everyone would fight to hold me. Remember the time when I was someone's favorite. Remember a time when someone tucked me in at night and kissed me on the cheek. Remember a time when someone cared enough to put me on a ruffled dress and brush my hair and pull it up into a ponytail and tell me that I was beautiful. I look at the reflection of my tears as they bring darkness to the pink t-shirt that covers my skin and wipe them away with both of my hands, then rub the wetness on the outside of my gray sweat pants. I gather my loose hair and pull it up into a ponytail. I inhale deeply, trying to give my body the oxygen it needs to come alive. Then I exhale slowly. I look at the single razor blade on the bathroom counter, covered with a thin piece of white paper, like it is strong enough to protect someone from the sharpness that lies within its cover and I pick it up. I walk back into the dim lit room, and sit on the edge of the bed. I remove the cover and let it hit the floor. I try and remember the moment that my beauty became untouchable and I can't. I'm so unsure of my faded beauty. Maybe I gave it to love as a sacrifice or offering in hopes that love would have me. Because even

I know that love won't commit one way. But love is as blurred to me as beauty because it does not look or feel the same to me anymore. Reality has replaced my childhood fantasies of a majestic love. Love left me alone in the cold without a fight. When did love transcend into all of this hurt and pain inside of me. I just want to leave. I wanna go where love is the air that covers me. And all of my mistakes fade and the light of God shines on my face, and I not only see my beauty but I feel it. I place the sharp end of the blade against the inside of my left wrist, press down and feel the sting as warmth of blood starts to stream as I continue to cut across my vein. I cry as I do the same to my other wrist. Not because it hurts, but because I don't feel anything. I pray that God truly sees my heart and truly sees that my soul was full of good intentions. I look at my teddy bear, and remember that there was a time someone favored me, and smile.

"Ebonee, Ebonee baby open your eyes for me!" I hear a familiar woman's voice.

I open my eyes and the white light is so bright that it hurts my eyes to keep them open so I have to close them.

"That's great. You're going to be okay." The familiar voice says as I feel my body being rolled somewhere, before everything goes black again.

I open my eyes and adjust my sight and I see Kioni asleep in the chair, right beside my hospital bed. I move my fingers and it wakes her because she fell asleep holding my hand.

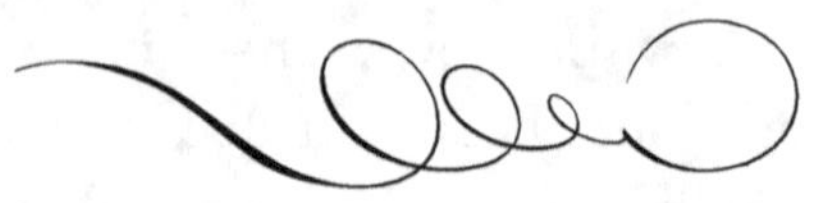

360 Degrees

"I didn't want to change the mood earlier, but how are things coming along with Ebonee?" I ask Kioni as she hands me two plates and I place them in the dishwasher from tonight's dinner, then close and turn it on.

"They moved her to Memorial. You know the procedure. I want to thank both of you for the flowers and beautiful words of encouragement you guys sent to her room. It really lifted her spirits to know that there are people in the world that really care if she stays in it, mistakes and all." Kioni says with a slight sigh.

"There's no need to thank us. You know that's what real women do, support and uplift each other!" Dianah says with a slight shrug of her shoulders.

"It's unfortunate that you have to go through so many fake ones to find them." Kioni says while she pours the last of the second bottle of chilled wine into the carafe.

"Who you tellin'…" I say and we all laugh.

"So how is the move working out for you?" I asked Dianah as I break her eyes away from their gaze at Ramona, as she engages in a distant conversation being held on the screened-in porch.

"It's amazing. I love waking up to Ramona's smell, feel, and voice every morning. And I am comforted all day by the fact that I get to come home, crawl into bed, and fall asleep to the same." Dianah says with a soft smile and looks at Ramona one more time, then back at me.

"We should be asking you the same thing missy." Kioni says with that "spill it" expression on her face.

"Yeah, how are things now that N'dia moved in with you and Cameron?" Dianah waits for my reply.

"We are all on cloud 9." I say, then think about the way Cameron and I woke her up this morning. Me, in front of her kissing, sucking, touching, and entering places with my fingers and tongue. And Cameron doing the same thing to her from the back of her at the same time.

"Earth to Raven!" Dianah snaps her fingers in front of me breaking my thoughts.

"I'm not even going to ask where you went." Kioni says and we all brandish devilish grins of our own, and walk out of the kitchen and rejoin everyone else on the porch.

"Wow!" Ramona says, and everyone but Dianah, Kioni and I laugh.

"What did we miss baby?" Dianah questions Ramona as she takes her place beside her and I take mine between Cameron and N'dia.

"Ramona asks Cameron to explain what monogamously polyamorous means, and Cameron said that you would be the better one to do that. And no sooner than she said it, you walked out." Chase fills us in as Kioni runs her fingers through her hair while she speaks.

"I see." I say, then I take a sip of wine from the glass N'dia hands me.

"I know what polyamory is, but I have never heard the term "monogamous" used in front of it. I hope you don't mind my curiosity?" Ramona states in a pleasant and sincere tone.

"Not at all." I say. Then I begin to share what it means to me. "I know that when people hear the word monogamous, they tend to think that the word alone implies a one on one relationship. But to me, monogamous means isolated commitment. Polyamorous as we all know means to love more than one person, which I do. I say, then I look at both of my lovers for a moment, then go back to my theory. "Now although I agree that we are all beings that are capable of sharing our bodies, minds, hearts, and souls with a multitude of people. I am and so are Cameron and N'dia, might I add, are very possessive and territorial women. So the idea of either of them sleeping with someone outside of our triad does not sit well with any of us. So we all agree on sharing a monogamous/isolated commitment with each other." I say, then I take another sip of my wine.

"That would bring our relationship to an end quickly!" N'dia says with her eyebrow arched and takes a sip of her wine as to wash down the unacceptable.

"So to make sure I understand you clearly, you guys are saying that you would break up over outside sex without forgiveness even though you believe it's possible to love and be attracted to multiple people?"

"Without a doubt, that would be the ultimate form of disrespect because being monogamously poly is about so much more than the sex, at least for us. We share everything with each other so if one of us stepped outside of the bond of trust that we have built with each other, we are going against everything this relationship stands for, and that is add to, inspire, uplift, and growing together!" Cameron says and looks me and N'dia in our eyes, letting hers tell us that she would never do that to us.

"Hell, but that is how it should be in any healthy relationship." Chase says as she kisses Kioni with tenderness.

"Most people look at situations like the one Raven, Cameron and I share and think about the sex, or try to figure out the placement that we all have in each other's lives. I don't know how many times I have heard the phrase "Hell naw girl, uh uh, I could never come second to any other bitch". And I laugh to myself first of all because I would never refer or any other woman as a bitch. And secondly, because I never have felt or been treated as a second to anyone. I have to intellectually stimulating, confident, free-spirited, and beautiful women in the world that see me for who I am, flaws and all. And they truly adore me as much as I adore them!" N'dia says, then leans in kisses me on my lips softly as Cameron takes a drink from her glass.

"I love her even more right now!" Kioni says and Dianah and I crack up laughing because the both of us know that the fact the N'dia just kissed me in front of everyone without hesitation is what she likes.

I look around at the smiles that cover the faces of my friends and lovers. I inhale the intimacy of this moment. I see the changes that have taken place in each of our lives. Some in private walls of our minds and others in like memories that we will all share forever and I exhale a breath that is full of growth. I close my eyes for a second and enjoy the safety of being among friends, and then I open them.

"Let's toast." I say and everyone moves in a little closer to each other and we all raise our glasses towards heaven.

"To letting go of those you must, holding on to the ones you can, and enjoying the journey along the way!"

ABOUT AUTHOR

"I think that every great feat is created from one simple thought. So after romanticizing about the idea of a world full of women that find beauty, strength, love, and a common sisterhood with each other, instead of viewing each other as rivals or inferior in some form or another if we give the slightest compliment to one another. I found myself thinking how easy the uncommon could become common if women could stop focusing on all the things that make us different from sexuality, race, genetics, and cultural backgrounds. That we would be able to see the truth, which is that every woman travels a different path in life but we are all connected by the same emotions."